Cactus
Cavalier

Cactus Cavalier

Norman A. Fox

Thorndike Press • Chivers Press
Thorndike, Maine USA   Bath, Avon, England

This Large Print edition is published by Thorndike Press, USA
and by Chivers Press, England.

Published in 1996 in the U.S. by arrangement
with Richard C. Fox.

Published in 1996 in the U.K. by arrangement with
the author's estate.

U.S.   Hardcover   0-7862-0651-9   (Western Series Edition)
U.K.   Hardcover   0-7451-4755-0   (Chivers Large Print)
U.K.   Softcover   0-7451-4802-6   (Camden Large Print)

Thorndike Large Print ® Western Series.

The text of this Large Print edition is unabridged.
Other aspects of the book may vary from the original edition.

Set in 16 pt. News Plantin by Juanita Macdonald.

H348799470

Printed in Great Britain on permanent paper.

British Library Cataloguing in Publication Data available

Library of Congress Catalog Card Number: 95-91006
ISBN: 0-7862-0651-9 (lg. print : hc)

For
ROBERT

CONTENTS

CONTENTS

This town, this Swayback, had grown from the grass roots of the virgin plain. Spawned in the trampled dust of empire, its birth throes had been part of a mighty cross-current, that south to north migration of the Texas cattle-man, that exodus which had brought the long-horn and violence and the Rebel's uncon-quered yell to Montana's hundred hills. This had been its inception, a bit of Texas trans-planted. This had shaped its destiny, too, for cattle had created a new kingdom here in the northland, and the men of the whang-leather breed left their mark upon whatever they made. There was a sprinkling of border Span-ish in the talk of Swayback's streets. There was the remembrance of a warmer clime in the batwing style of its saloon doors. Yet Swayback was Swayback; its personality was its own. The lusty infant had grown to the gawky youngster, serene and thoughtful in its milder moments, wild and unpredictable when the mood was upon it.

These things Larkin sensed when he topped the last ridge to the east to look down upon the great bowl of tawny rangeland which Swayback centred. Distance softened the town, dimming the ugliness of hasty architecture, erasing the squalor of aimless, straggling streets. Viewed thus, Swayback was like a hundred towns through which Larkin's trail had taken him, but he looked upon this scatteration of buildings with kinder eyes, for here was home. Two things a man possessed of no kin might cling to: the love of a woman, and the love for the place to which his wanderings always returned him. Remembering this, Larkin smiled.

He might have hurried now, for the sun was at its highest and he was hungry, but he drew some strange delight from this lingering contemplation of trail's end. Overhead the sky's arched blueness bent to the far horizon, merging with the deeper blue of the distant Silver Belt range. Strange how a man was always conscious of clouds in this vast, open land; they had kept Larkin company across miles of loneliness. To-day, though, his attention was drawn to the land, and to the shimmering steel rails that caught the sunlight and span it in twin strands across the basin and through Swayback and beyond it. There'd been no railroad when last he'd looked from this ridge; he wasn't sure that the change was to his liking.

He was a man used to his own solitary whimsies; he had followed a calling that had kept him apart from lasting friendships. He had learned to rely upon his own reasoning and his own instinct, and, just for a moment, he was seized with an impulse to turn his horse and head away from Swayback. He recognised this as a fear, and he tried then to put his finger on it, but it eluded him, and it stood no test of logic that he could give it. It had, he supposed, something to do with the difference here that met the eye, yet all things changed; he himself was not the man who had once ridden away. But because there was a fear, he fought it down, banishing it from his consciousness. This was habit with him, this putting his back to any dread. He smiled again, and said aloud, "You damn' fool. You come a thousand miles, and you get buck fever within sight of old Swayback. . . ."

The town had indeed changed. He saw that when he came riding into the outskirts an hour later; Swayback was grown and was like a remembered friend, familiar of face but touched by the years. On the outskirts were the better dwellings, and among these Larkin recognised the house of Sheldon Abbott, a two-storied frame structure, its white paint kept new, a quietly impressive building, neither too large nor too opulent, yet commanding attention. The house was like the man, Larkin reflected,

11

and remembered Sheldon Abbott, Swayback's first mayor, without rancour, grateful to him because Abbott had kept this one bit of Swayback as it had been.

Beyond these dwellings, Larkin came into a main street that had not even existed in the past, a new row of mercantile stores, a blacksmith shop, a livery, a saloon. There was a staid respectability here; he could see it in the unhurried steps of bonneted women, the careful courtesy of soft-spoken men, and he found this reassuring. Not far distant was the red, low-roofed railroad depot and the tracks which bisected the town, and beyond these was old Santone Street which had been the main thoroughfare in days gone by. With no conscious prompting, Larkin threaded his way to the region south of the tracks.

The Amarillo House, first of Swayback's hotels, still stood on Santone Street, and Larkin racked his horse before the high false front of the place, shouldered his war-sack and crossed the boardwalk to the stuffy lobby. The men who sat dispiritedly upon the horsehair sofas in this scanty space gave him little more than a show of casual curiosity; the clerk was an old man remembered from the yesterdays, but there was no recognition in the fellow's eyes. He saw Larkin as another rider, a tall, wide-shouldered man made lean and limber by the saddle, a man brown of face and bleak of eye, with a ragged shock of black hair showing beneath the flat-brimmed Mormon hat he happened to be wearing to-day. Larkin wore no guns, and some would have found that strange, but the clerk's glance was brief. He passed over a key and said, "Number seven. Last door to your left at the street end of the hall."

Larkin put down his name and gave a long thought to the address to put after it, then wrote in a firm, bold hand, "Dodge City, Kansas."

"My horse is outside," he said. "See that he's stabled and grained."

"Sure," said the clerk, and Larkin had reached the head of the stairs before the gusty ejaculation came from the man at the desk below. He knew then, did Larkin, that the fellow had seen his name, and he knew, too, that the name would shortly go the rounds of the town, borne on the swift feet of rumour, carried with gusto and colour and great elaboration. He had anticipated this, and with no delight; he had even thought of subterfuges to avoid it. But a man couldn't deny his name or his reputation in his own home town.

The room to the front of the building was as Larkin had known it would be before he opened its creaking door — a replica of a hun-

13

dred such rooms in a hundred such towns. The carpet was worn to the thread in many places; the pine bureau with its inevitable pitcher and bowl stood precariously upon three legs; the bed was chipped, the blankets uninviting. There was a chair in one corner, a fly-speckled calendar upon the wall. This and nothing more. Larkin sloshed water into the basin and washed the grime of travel from himself, rasping his hand across his cheeks afterwards and deciding that the shave he'd gotten by this morning's campfire would do him until another sunrise.

This done, he moved to the single window, hoisted the cracked shade and had his look down upon old Santone Street. Weathered buildings shouldered each other to the limits of his vision; there were wooden awnings and gnawed hitch-rails, and twin boardwalks paralleled the tawny dust of the street. Directly across the way was a newer building, flamboyantly fronted and bearing the legend, THE FANDANGO — NICK DIAMOND, *Prop*. From here, in the hush of the early afternoon, he could hear the swelling murmur of many voices, the steady beat of a tuneless piano, and he found this strange; for the saloons should be locked in a sleepy lethargy at this hour. There were other saloons on Santone Street, he noticed; many more than he could remember. The old mercantile store, for instance, had had a pair of batwings put into its front recently, and there were at least half a dozen horses racked before it.

Below him a dog dozed in the dust of the street, and a boy of around twelve played some aimless, silent game of his own creation. He studied the boy, the only human in sight at the moment, seeing him as ragged and underfed, and, when the sun sent dancing shards of light, he observed that the boy wore a pair of spurs upon naked heels. Larkin smiled at that, and, still smiling, grew thoughtful. For now he knew the scope of the change that had come over Swayback, and he wondered what mental blindness had closed his eyes to a pattern that was so old and familiar.

This was a town divided in two, now; the railroad tracks made the line of demarcation, and this region south of the tracks, this Santone Street, was of one world, its spirit personified by the flamboyant Fandango, just as the staid house of Sheldon Abbott spoke of another kind of life to the north of the tracks. There were the town builders, the men who had put up the first structures in Swayback and brought a semblance of order in the wake of the trampling herds. But there was a new breed of men here, too, the breed of the Fandango, and this was their street. True, there had been violence in Swayback before, the exuberant violence of Texans long held to the rigours of the trail, a boyish exultation let loose at trail's end and taking strange forms. But the kind of violence that would emanate from such places as Santone Street was of another kind, a studied violence made of an age-old challenge of one breed of men to another.

That was it, and Larkin remembered a parade of towns — Abilene, Wichita, Dodge City, Tombstone, Julesburg. . . . These also had been born in the dust of empire and had drawn two elements and found a need for a quick and merciless law. And, so thinking, he tasted the irony of having put a certain kind of life behind him only to find that the turn of the trail had brought him back to his starting point. He had remembered an Eden and returned to it, but the serpent was already here. Then his gaze lifted over the false fronts to the range beyond, and he was reassured; for that was where his destiny lay. Old habits of thinking had gotten a hard grip on him for the moment. Santone Street was the place where he would spend only these few hours that he might need in Swayback.

And then it happened.

First there was the roar of a shot from within the Fandango, a blatant burst of sound that

16

was muffled in part by the walls and by a sudden discordant crash of the piano keys. The many voices inside the saloon blended together and rose to a new, high note, throaty and primitive. Across the way, Larkin saw the batwings give to the thrust of a man's body; a fellow came out through them, a big, blond giant of a man, hatless and with a tousled yellow mane. A man at each of the giant's elbows propelled him forward. They gave the fellow a sudden last shove; he went stumbling across the boardwalk and tripped over its edge to go sprawling in the dust and then he was hauling himself to his feet, a wild and unchecked anger in his attitude.

The giant wore no gun. This Larkin saw at once, for at the first signs of violence he instantly took to weighing the means of violence. The two who had thrown the giant from the Fandango carried weapons, though, but they made no move towards them; the need was not apparent yet. In one hand the giant clutched what appeared to Larkin to be a few playing-cards. With his free hand the fellow scooped a rock from the street and hurled it straight at one of the pair that had expelled him — a lean and wiry man with his face shadowed by the wide brim of a sombrero. The rock struck the lean man on the shoulder, swerving him off balance, and the second man got his gun into his hand, the street shuddering to the roar of it.

Some inkling of his nearness to death must have percolated through the giant's anger then; he stumbled backwards across the street, stumbled to the protection of a water barrel on the boardwalk, just at the rim of Larkin's vision. But now Larkin's attention was drawn to the other two creatures in this tableau — the dozing dog and the bare-footed boy. The dog had come to sudden life, *ki-yi*-ing away in a mad scramble, and the boy was running, too. But fear had blinded the youngster, and he ran in the wrong direction, cutting diagonally towards the Fandango, but he might have made it to safety if he hadn't tripped over those spurs he wore.

The wild cry of warning that welled in Larkin's throat died in an agonised gurgle of sound. He was a man paralysed in that moment, thinking of many things, remembering his own guns carefully stowed away in his war-sack, making an estimation of the time it would take to get them into his hands and knowing there wasn't time enough. He could only stand and watch, and thus he saw the boy die, going down to writhe in the dust. He had run directly into the path of fire, and he would run no more.

The silence came down then like something

tangible, something that gripped the street and held it until it even hurt to listen. There was the boy lying there unmoving, and the giant coming out from behind the barrel, a look of infinite pain and surprise upon his broad face, and the two before the Fandango, both with smoking guns in their hands, but holding them as though they'd suddenly grown hot. The giant stowed the cards he held into his shirt pocket, performing this simple act as though he were unaware of it, and yet as though it were the most important thing in the world. He came out into the street, his boots stirring up little explosions of dust, and he picked up the fallen boy and cradled him in his arms, the two at the Fandango only staring at him.

Then the silence was gone again; men came pouring from the Fandango and from the hotel, converging around the giant until the street was black and alive with them. Larkin crossed the room and took the stairs, and when he came elbowing through the crowd, someone was saying, "Here comes Hobbs now. He must have heard the gunfire."

Matt Hobbs had been Swayback's first marshal, and it came now to Larkin as a surprise that the old man still held that post. The years had put their weight on Hobbs when Larkin had first known him; now the man was even more stooped, and the silver of his shaggy hair and eyebrows had lost some of its lustre. Hobbs had a limp to him as he forced his way through the crowd, and his voice was old and tired when he spoke.

"The Davis kid, eh?" he said. "Who did it?"

The Fandango man who'd been struck by the rock nudged back his sombrero with his free hand, thereby revealing a lean, saturnine face, blue-black of jowl, though no beard stubble showed. He seemed to remember the gun he held, for now he cased it. "Reckon I did, Matt," he said.

Hobbs' face hardened, the wrinkles between his tufted eyebrows bunching. "Ye've gone gunning for children, Kinsella?"

Kinsella shrugged. "We had a ruckus in the Fandango. Sorenson, there, got mouthy when his luck at poker went against him, and he called our house-man a cheat. We had to throw the big Swede out, and he took to hurling rocks. The kid just happened to get in the way of the shooting."

The giant Scandinavian, seen this closely, appeared to be little more than a boy. He opened his mouth, the protest he intended to make plain in his china-blue eyes, but before he could speak another man elbowed towards Hobbs, and this man said, "I saw it all, Matt. Sorenson provoked my boys to gunplay. You'd better lock him up for disturbing the peace."

He won Larkin's quick attention, this man, not for what he'd said, but for the way he'd said it. There'd been surety behind his words, the surety of a man who knows his power and expects others to recognise it. He had put the right shade of deference in his speech to Matt Hobbs; he had made a suggestion, but his phrasing had been the thin veneer that covered a command. Yet there was nothing formidable about his appearance. As tall as Larkin, he was slight of shoulder and wasp-waisted, and his face, effeminately handsome, gave no suggestion of strength. Black broadcloth garbed him; his boots were hand-stitched, and his waistcoat spotlessly white. A man saw such dandies in the frontier metropolises; Cheyenne or Denver or San Antonio would have made a proper setting for him; here in the dust of Swayback's street he looked out of place. He was Nick Diamond, and somehow Larkin knew that before Hobbs spoke.

"I'll jail Sorenson, yes, Diamond," Hobbs said, his mouth drawn to a stubborn line. "But I'll also jail Sig Kinsella and that other plug-ugly of yours. The Davis kid is dead, and if it wasn't an accident, somebody will swing for this."

Diamond smiled a soft and bewitching

smile. "The evidence hardly warrants anything but a charge of disturbing the peace. I'll post bond for my men right now. Here, a hundred dollars should more than cover it."

The stubbornness went out of Hobbs' mouth, and he was older for the change. "Very well, Diamond," he said wearily. "If I drag your boys off to jail, you'll go to Judge Bragg and have them out in half an hour anyway. I know that. Come along, Sorenson, and bring the kid's body. There'll be a hearing in justice court this evening. Have your boys there, Diamond." His ancient eyes swept the crowd. "Anybody see the ruckus?"

"Yes," said Larkin. "I saw it."

He was one of many up until that moment; he'd been cloaked by the anonymity of the crowd, but Matt Hobbs' eyes went to him now, and so did every one else's, and Hobbs was a man seeing the shape of a nebulous hope. "Larkin!" he cried. "Dave Larkin! Not five minutes ago somebody told me ye'd ridden into town. Joshing me, they were; said you'd come back to take my badge. Son, you're welcome to it — and right now!"

Larkin said, "No, Matt. I've quit that kind of game. I've only one day to spend in Swayback."

Nick Diamond bestowed his smile upon Larkin and said, "Then you won't be wasting your time by staying for the hearing, amigo. I'd advise you not to bother with it."

Larkin turned, turned slowly, and his gaze met Diamond's, and in that moment the enmity between them was born. As yet it had no basis in actuality; there wasn't the sort of challenge in Diamond's words to stir a man to sudden fury, but Larkin, looking at the man, knew that they'd been born to oppose each other, and he knew that Diamond recognised this same truth. It was that way always; there were the two breeds, and when they came against each other it was flint against stone.

Larkin said, "I'm not in *that* much of a hurry, mister. I'll likely be on hand to-night."

Yet even as he spoke he knew the old regret; a man schemed to put his yesterdays behind him, but the pattern shaped itself once more and was there for the facing. And because he didn't want to face it, Larkin remembered the business that had brought him here; and he put his back to Diamond, a slow, contemptuous gesture, and spoke to Hobbs.

"I'm here to see Amy Pierce, Matt," he said. "Would you know whether she happens to be in town to-day?"

Hobbs found it hard to speak; there was the moment of hesitation, and a stammer to his tongue when the words did come. "Amy — ?" he repeated. "You're here to see Amy?"

"Why not?" said Larkin, and smiled.

"She's here," Hobbs said. "She's living in town now, of course. You'll find her at Sheldon Abbott's house. Remember the place? Out near the north edge of town."

"I see," Larkin said. "I see."

He turned away from Hobbs and began elbowing through the crowd towards the Amarillo House, and it came to him now that he knew what it was he had feared there on the ridge overlooking Swayback — the fear that had had no name. It had been with him for a long time, that fear, but he'd kept it closeted in the part of his mind where a man stores the things he doesn't wish to bring to the light of consciousness. Two things he'd had to cling to: the love of a woman and the love for the place to which his wanderings had returned him. But those two things were intertwined, separate parts of a single whole, and the town had changed, and the woman belonged now to another man. He had, he reflected, followed a fool's trail to a fool's finish. He had come to Swayback too late.

"Larkin's back," Sheldon Abbott said, and watched the way those words took with his wife.

It was the hour when the shadow legions came marching stealthily down from the Silver Belts and the town mellowed to the touch of night, the lamp-lighting hour, but Sheldon Abbott preferred to sit in the gathering gloom. He had worked his wheel-chair into the big living-room which fronted his frame house; he had grown quite adept at manipulating the chair in the six months he had been confined to it. Now he sat with his hands folded in his blanket-wrapped lap, a tall, spare, carefully groomed man with a long wedge-like face, made longer by the black side-burns he affected. A cripple's helplessness had changed no facet of his personality; he shaved by the clock and kept his tie properly knotted, and there was always an odour of talc and astringents about him. He had been Swayback's first mayor and he still held that post, though he was little more than thirty. A young land called for young blood.

Amy Abbott had been gone an unwarranted time on some shopping expedition to the main street; he had heard her bustling about the building upon her return, and he had taken his time deciding how to tell her. She stood now in the doorway to the living-room, her bonnet still dangling from her arm, her black hair parted in the middle and drawn to a tight bun at the nape of her neck. Hers was a face that was almost classic in its perfection, but she was voluptuously full-bodied; she was made of ice and fire, a frozen flame. She said now, "I know, Sheldon. I heard over at the store. Every busybody in town seems to have appointed herself to carry the news to me."

That took the edge from whatever macabre triumph he had hoped to derive from this moment, and his second disappointment came when she didn't ask how *he* knew. He had built an air of omniscience about him; he had made it a part of a politician's careful trade; even Amy showed no surprise at the things he always managed to learn.

Amy said, "You still hate him, don't you, Sheldon?"

He shrugged, but before he could speak she said, "Of course you do. About the last thing he did before leaving this town seven years ago was to duck you in the horse trough over on Santone Street with half the town watching. He'd have done better for himself if he'd put a bullet in you. Pain, you could forgive.

Humiliation has eaten at you all these years. When you trample on some men's dignity, you get little satisfaction. But that doesn't hold true for the Sheldon Abbotts."

She crossed to a low stool beside his chair and settled herself upon it, clasping his folded hands in hers. At moments like this their eternal sparring was done with, and they were very close to each other. She said softly, "You've nothing to worry about, Sheldon. He was only to be here for a day. When Matt Hobbs told him where he'd find me, he went back into the Amarillo House, and he's only shown himself once since — to get a bite to eat. His horse will be rested by sundown and he'll ride out. You can take a woman's word for that."

Abbott said, "He's become quite a hero since you saw him last."

"For schoolgirls," she said. "And for the people of small achievement who always have to look to somebody else to see themselves as they'd like to be. No, Sheldon. I was sixteen years old when he left. I'm twenty-three now — and Mrs. Sheldon Abbott."

He lifted a hand to her hair and stroked it gently, yet there was a certain possessiveness in the gesture. He said, "You're right, my dear. I do hate him. Yet I don't want him to ride away. We must keep him here in Swayback, and we must hurry if we are to do so. It is sundown now."

Her eyes were dark, and sometimes she had a way of dropping a curtain behind them; but now she let stark surprise show. "Keep him here!"

"He has acquired certain talents since he left us," Sheldon Abbott said. "He has made a name for himself at a strange and terrifying trade, and Swayback needs a man with his skill. You see, my dear, I have to remember myself as Sheldon Abbott, a man — and a sorry spectacle of a man these days — but I also have to remember that I'm the mayor of Swayback. It's the town I'm thinking of to-night. The town and what Dave Larkin could do for it."

She knew exactly what he meant, and he saw the knowledge in her eyes. That was their way; they played with words, but they never fooled each other. She said, "But what will keep him here, Sheldon? He's not a boy now, to be twisted around anybody's finger; he's a man. Who will change his mind if he's determined to ride away?"

"You will, my dear," said Sheldon Abbott. "You will."

"S'pose ye heard that Dave Larkin hit town to-day," Marshal Matthew Hobbs said.

28

He stood in the doorway of the office that bore the legend: JUDGE JOSHUA X. BRAGG, *Justice of the Peace*, the largest of the rooms in a creaky, frame building on the main street which housed the town's officials. His own cubby-hole was down the hall, but there was in Matt Hobbs the need for companionship and another man's wisdom to-night, and that need had sent him across this threshold.

This was the room where a hearing would be held later in the evening; a low railing separated a section of chairs from a spur-scarred desk with a witness-stand beside it. Behind the desk, Judge Bragg tilted precariously in a swivel chair, his boots crossed expansively upon the desk top. Now, made aware that he was not alone in the room, Bragg came to a more decorous position.

A large and pudgy man, given to flowing ties and staid clothing, Bragg had let his silvery mane grow almost to his shoulders, and he affected the moustache and skimpy goatee of a gentleman of the South. Since his face was puffy and red-veined and his nose was bulbous, the result was somewhat incongruous, but this might be truly said of him: he was an expert judge of whisky and horse-flesh, and his accent, though exaggerated, likely came from Texas. A scant two months before, Swayback had seen him for the first time; he had ridden in on a sorry excuse for a mule; he had put himself into the town hall with a glib tongue and a persuasive personality, and he had endeared himself with small boys and old ladies. He carried a handsome walking-stick — it lay upon his desk at the moment — and rumour told it that a shining sword was encased therein.

As Hobbs came down the aisle between the chairs, Bragg said, "Greetings, suh. Yes, I've heard of the timely arrival of your local legend. But you, suh, had better be turning your mind to other affairs. 'Pears you have a tiger by the tail."

"Meaning the Sorenson-Diamond hearing to-night?" Hobbs asked, for this was precisely what had brought him here, and the thought was easily come by.

"Decidedly, suh. You can't very well find the Fandango crowd guilty to-night without lifting the lid and letting the merry blue blazes come bubbling out. Yet your alternative, suh, is to punish Sorenson, even if the evidence indicates that he was as blameless as a man might be under such circumstances."

"I know," Hobbs said dismally and seated himself in the witness-chair. "Diamond has taken over south of the tracks. The best I've been able to do is keep him there. Cross him now, and he'll try taking over the town. And who is there to stop him?"

"I, suh, have given due consideration to to-night's problem," Bragg announced and let a moment of silence give proper emphasis to his words. "And I, suh, have found your solution for you."

There was in Matt Hobbs an envy of this man; he would have given much for Bragg's easy way of shrugging aside worry, of taking a problem apart and seeing its separate pieces for what they were worth. Yet he knew that the difference in their make-up was that Bragg never let a conscience stand between him and wisdom; he was a cutter of Gordian knots, this Bragg, by virtue of a healthy respect for his own skin, plus a bland disregard for the finer aspects of book law.

And yet: "I'm listening to ye," said Matt Hobbs.

"Then, suh, we shall conduct our hearing in the manner of my old friend, Judge Roy Bean, the man who made himself the law west of the Pecos, and who frequently consulted me before rendering important decisions. We, suh, shall arrange to find Banjo Sorenson guilty of misdemeanour. The death of the Davis boy will have to be put down as an accident of nobody's contrivance — which it appears to have been. Nick Diamond will be satisfied, for the Fandango crowd will be ab-

31

solved of guilt. But I, suh, shall not sentence Sorenson to our calaboose. Instead I shall order him to be out of town before sunrise, and I shall stipulate that he is not to return. Sorenson will resent that, suh, but you will carry out the order of the co't. For by doing so, you will save Banjo Sorenson's life."

"Meaning that ye think Diamond will send Kinsella gunning for the Swede if Sorenson ever walks the street free?"

Bragg snapped his pudgy fingers. "*That,* suh, is all Diamond cares about Banjo Sorenson, dead or alive. No, Diamond will doubtless have no further interest in our Scandinavian friend, after the hearing. But Sorenson is in Swayback to make a search, suh; and when he finds the man he seeks, Banjo Sorenson will die."

Hobbs' tufted eyebrows bunched, and he said, "Ye know something about him, I see. Ye've drawn talk out of that big Swede since you came here, which is more than anybody else has done. Just what are ye driving at, Bragg?"

"Sorenson hails from the timber country, suh. Those shoulders and arms come from swinging a double-bitted axe, or I've lost my sense of perception. It happens, suh, that I've had some considerable experience at felling timber in the past — as an overseer, of course.

The boy doubtless recognised me as a kindred spirit in an alien land. For it is only a year or so since Sorenson fetched his young sister with him from Minnesota and took up a bit of land to the east of here. That, suh, I've had from his own lips."

"A sister, ye say? But he came here alone."

"His sister is dead, suh. Sorenson left her alone one day while he went into the hills to drag down poles for a new corral. When he returned, he found tragedy. There'd been a visitor, you see, some passing rider, and there'd been a struggle. A bullet had finished the girl, but whether the man had shot her to keep her from identifying him later, or whether she'd used a gun on herself — afterwards — Sorenson did not say. Do you understand me, suh?"

Hobbs' face had gone ashy grey; in him was all the anger of a frontier man who hears tell of the one crime for which there is no forgiving. He said hoarsely, "Yes, I understand ye! And Sorenson is here looking for that man?"

Bragg nodded. "Such sign as he was able to cut, suh, pointed towards Swayback."

"Then where's the danger for him?" Hobbs asked. "If he finds his man, the whole town will help hang the jigger. And I'll put my badge away and pull on the rope myself."

"Think, suh!" Bragg counselled. "Will Sorenson come to others for help when he finds his man? No, suh; he'll try wreaking his own vengeance, and he'll likely die. He's had no training with a gun; he told me so himself. He scarcely ever carries one. No, suh, if you want that boy to stay alive, and he's a good boy who deserves to live, you'll have to send him out of town by the law's order. He'll never go otherwise. And to-night's hearing will give you your opportunity, suh, with Sorenson getting no inkling of the true reason why we'll be banishing him from our midst."

Hobbs said unsteadily, "I've gotten too old for my job; I've known it for a long time, and every day gives me a new reason for knowing it better. My resignation's been on file for weeks; if only I hadn't been fool enough to let Sheldon Abbott talk me into promising to stay on until a man could be found to take my place. If Dave Larkin was looking for a badge —"

"Poof, suh!" Judge Bragg interjected, and snapped his fingers again. "You attach too much importance to this Larkin. I, suh, was once with considerable skill at his trade." He sighed and regarded his expansive stomach. "In my younger years, of course."

Hobbs was recalled to reality by a sudden remembrance; he hoisted himself from the chair and limped towards the gate in the low railing. "I've got prisoners to feed," he said. "Sorenson might as well hear the worst on a full stomach. And Crad Conover is likely bellowing to the jail's rafters. I'd better get on over to the Chinaman's."

"So Dave Larkin's back in town," Crad Conover said when Matt Hobbs had fetched two trays from the restaurant into the long log and frame building that was Swayback's jail. In one of the two occupied cells giving off the shadowy corridor, Banjo Sorenson munched stolidly on the food, but Conover, jailed for rustling, was of a mind to talk. He stood leaning against the bars of his cell door, a high-shouldered youngster, handsome in a wildling sort of way, and arrogant even in this imprisonment. His garb was black, the drabness of it relieved by pearl and silver.

A day's excitement had put a heavy strain on Matt Hobbs, and the marshal said irritably, "Have you had visitors? Or do ye Conovers have the gift of seeing through walls?"

"I can see part of the street from the window of this bird-cage," Conover said. "And I can hear talk. The whole town's buzzing with it. Who do they think Larkin is, anyway? He was a forty-a-month-and-found cowpoke when he left this range, a waddy of

35

Cultus Pierce's who didn't have any more brains than to make calf's eyes at his boss's daughter. Any change that's come over him since is all in folk's heads. He don't stack up so almighty high!"

Sharp annoyance drove Hobbs to a taunt. "They'll tell you different in the Kansas trail towns," he said. "But likely ye'll only learn when you learn for yourself. Maybe Larkin is taking over my job, Conover. Maybe King Conover will think twice about raiding this town to take his kid brother out of the calaboose when Dave Larkin is rodding the law."

Crad Conover laughed contemptuously. "King will tear this jail apart when he's of a mind to," he said. "If Dave Larkin's here, the job will be just that much more interesting for the King. You're whistling in the dark, old-timer."

The old weariness put its weight on Matt Hobbs' shoulders again. Truly Judge Bragg had drawn a clear parallel when he'd talked of Swayback's law having a tiger by the tail. The trouble was that there were half a dozen tigers, and one man was having a time for himself hanging on to all of them.

"Finish up your grub, Banjo," he said, turning to the giant Scandinavian's adjoining cell. "It's almost time to head over for the hearing."

"Dave Larkin rode into Swayback to-day," the man announced as he approached a huddled group high in the Silver Belt foothills. Here the flickering wash of a small and smokeless fire high-lighted the dozen bearded faces of the men who crouched around it; shadows danced restlessly on the bald face of a cliff behind them. A coffee-pot made soft, bubbling music, and King Conover, he-wolf of this high country, had a tin cup in his hand. Putting it down, he came to a stand, a big rocky man with none of his brother's litheness. Yet there was in his craggy features some hint of the kinship, some similarity in the flare of nostrils and breadth of forehead. Conover said, "I sent you to town to fetch supplies and to get word of Crad, mister. That's the news I'm wanting to hear."

The newcomer had lately quit the saddle of a sweat-lathered horse; the rigours of a long, hard ride had left him with an irritable aggressiveness. "Your grub is in the tow-sack," he said and dropped his burden. "I managed to talk to Crad to-day, through his cell window. Hobbs was busy trying to be seven places at once, and me'n the kid had quite a palaver. The date of the trial hasn't been set yet. Seems Swayback isn't in a hurry to use rope law on King Conover's kid brother. But I ain't sure the sign is right to tackle the town. They'll be expecting us, King."

"You go anywhere near the bank?"

The other shook his head. "Figgered it best to keep clear of that layout."

Conover sandpapered his chin with his stubby fingers. "Hmm," he murmured reflectively. "You say Dave Larkin's come home? There's only one kind of job in Swayback that would interest him these days."

The man who had fetched the news had nourished it along the trail, but it had turned out to have a mighty puny effect. Like all these long-riding men who followed King Conover's lead, he had a need for excitement, and he had known a certain disappointment because he had created no stir. But now he saw a new potentiality that might come from to-day's doings, and he said, "You ain't afraid of Larkin, are you, King?"

King Conover stiffened, but he was a man who kept anger for a time when the surge of it would serve him. "Afraid?" he said woodenly. "I reckon not. If Larkin takes the marshal's badge, he'll step on Nick Diamond's toes. That's bound to follow as night follows day. Diamond will take care of him. Mark my words."

On the plain that spread gently downwards

from the Silver Belts to Swayback town, the cluster of buildings that was the Boxed-C ranch headquarters squatted midway. Of these aimlessly huddled structures, one, the cook-shack, blazed with light at this early evening hour. Old Cultus Pierce was a man of many acres and many cattle, but he held to no pretence because of this, and he ate with his crew as he'd always done. While the dusk gathered, he washed himself at the bench beside the shack's door, and he had his leonine head muffled in the towel when one of his men shaped up out of the shadows.

"Dave Larkin's back, boss," the cowhand said. "Rode into town this noon."

Cultus put down the towel, soapy lather still streaking his leathery old face. "How's that?" he asked. "Dave back? Why, that's mighty good news! Mighty good!" But a new thought, striking him, brought a frown with it. "He'll be out to see me," he said, but he was thinking aloud and wasn't conscious that he'd spoken. "He was only a boy when he left; he's a man now; he won't hold it against me for what happened. Sure, he'll come and see me." He became conscious of the cowhand again. "You see Amy?"

"Sure," said the other. "I told her, like you said. She said, 'Tell my father that Sheldon and I will be more than happy to accept his

39

invitation to come to the ranch for dinner, Sunday.' "

" 'More than happy to accept his invitation!' " Cultus snorted. "What the hell kind of talk is that for a daughter to be using with her father? Pete, that gal of mine only married the mayor of a two-bit town, not the president of these United States. 'Happy to accept his invitation!' "

He turned thoughtful again; his moods were always transitory and usually violent; he was as elemental as the turning seasons that shaped the pattern of his life, as savage as a blizzard, as gentle as rain. "So Dave's come home," he mused. "Damned if I ain't anxious to see the kid."

"I've heard a heap of talk to-day about this Larkin gent, boss," Sig Kinsella said. He sat in Nick Diamond's office over the bar-room of the Fandango, a room furnished in the belief that an outward show of opulence carried a telling impression, and the light of an overhanging lamp gave an oily glow to his swarthy skin. "And what I've heard," he went on, "I don't like."

Diamond, leaning back in the chair that stood behind his desk, put himself just beyond the cone of light; long practice had made this a habit with him. Thus he could study Kinsella

40

without himself being studied, and he drew a certain amusement from the show of alarm in Kinsella's eyes. That was the way of the quick-triggered gentry, Diamond decided. Give them something to fight that they could see and line in their gunsights, and they were good men for their work. Give them something less tangible, and they took to worrying.

Diamond said, "Our concern is more immediate, Sig. It has to do with Banjo Sorenson and the hearing that will be starting mighty soon. And Mr. Larkin fits into our picture only to the extent that he makes a nuisance out of himself at the hearing. I've heard a lot about Larkin, too — so much that I've already discounted him. Swayback is too small for the size of *his* britches. You've got to have something of the calibre of Dodge City to interest the Dave Larkins. I'll not be surprised if he doesn't even stay for the hearing."

"But suppose he does?"

"Then we'll have to make a fool out of him. And also out of Sorenson. The Swede started a ruckus here in the Fandango because he thought he was being cheated. We've got to prove that he was playing the sore-head because he'd gotten a run of poor hands. That's the important thing, Sig. We're going to make an example out of Banjo Sorenson. We're

41

going to show Swayback that it isn't a good idea for a man to run off at the mouth about the way the games are conducted in the Fandango."

"How long, boss," asked Kinsella, "are we going to keep on playing it safe?"

"Until the sign is right, Sig. A few men like Sorenson squawking about us and that bunch north of the tracks will get righteous-minded and back up Hobbs in a little walk down this way that will have us packing our telescopes. But if we can hold the lid down a little longer, we'll be the ones who'll be moving — moving north of the tracks. We'll take over this town, Sig, and we'll run 'er wide open. How would you like to wind up wearing the marshal's badge?"

"I dunno," Kinsella said, the worry still in his eyes. "This Larkin —"

Diamond's handsome face hardened. "The trouble with you, Sig, is that you borrow trouble. You'll have to learn to take one thing at a time. Our problem to-night is the hearing. Larkin isn't a burr under our saddle blanket until he starts rubbing us. Then is when we start worrying about Dave Larkin."

He paused; his voice grew brittle as he spoke again. "And another thing, Sig. Keep away from Melody, do you understand? Don't even *think* what you've been thinking about her.

Oh, yes, I've seen it in your eyes. That girl came to the Fandango under her own terms, Sig. Those songs of hers bring us more trade than all our tables. Fools like to be reminded of home and love and all such wahoo. They come to hear her singing, and they stay to spend their money. You're not going to change that by having her pack her suitcase just because you can't get it through your thick head that she wants to be left alone."

A defiant anger lighted Kinsella's eyes, but only for a moment. "Whatever you say, boss," he agreed. "But this Larkin —"

In the room adjoining Nick Diamond's office to the left, the girl called Melody lay stretched upon her bed. This was her quarters, the only bit of Swayback that was hers. She had chosen it when Nick Diamond had offered her a room after she'd gone to work for him; he'd pointed out that the Amarillo House, across the way, was vermin-infested, and she'd already learned that first week that the newer hotels to the north of the tracks were not open to the girls of Diamond's Fandango. No, there'd been no insulting refusal; the vague mumblings of sundry desk clerks had been the more humiliating in their obliqueness.

Here she had a bed, and she'd made it pretty by sewing a canopy of sorts over it. She had a dresser, and its mirror was ringed with pictures and clippings from Eastern magazines that had found their way to Swayback. She had a chair and she had transformed it, too, making it gay with coloured cloth. She had brought brightness to the room, but she was blind to it to-night.

There was a knothole in the planking of the wall, and, since the bed was shoved up against the wall, the knothole was close to her ear as she stretched herself for rest before the arduous evening ahead. She'd long ago discovered that she could hear all that was said in Diamond's office through that knothole, so she'd plugged it with paper, for eavesdropping was not a pastime that brought her pleasure. But in spite of this she'd caught the name of Banjo Sorenson through the wall as Diamond and Sig Kinsella made talk in the office beyond, and she'd removed the wadding then and listened with all the license of a person who knows that a friend is in need.

She was golden-haired, this girl, and her face was sweet rather than pretty, and this same quality was in her songs and made her the most popular personage ever to cross the tiny stage that stood at the end of Diamond's bar-room below. There was about her an air of innocence, and yet she was not altogether naïve; a girl didn't sing her way

44

from one frontier honkytonk to another without learning that life had its sordid side.

Listening now, some of the sweetness went out of her and was replaced by worry and fear. She heard Dave Larkin's name, too, and of all the people who'd heard of Larkin's coming this day, she had been the least interested. Larkin meant nothing to her, yet Larkin became suddenly a name to cling to, for here was the faint embodiment of the only thing that approximated hope. And at last, when there came an end to listening because Kinsella and Diamond had quit the office, she meticulously stuffed the wadding back into the knothole, and then she took from the low-cut front of her dress a deck of cards. The dress was a concession to Diamond's insistence; she served his public only with song, but the dress drew customers, too. The cards in her hand, she fell to examining them as she'd done before. The deck was complete save for one hand, dealt at a poker table, a hand that had brought violence and death to Santone Street to-day.

Here, she knew, was a mighty weapon, forged by chance and capable of changing a man's fate to-night. That that man was Banjo Sorenson whetted her desperation. Yet this weapon was useless in her hands; she knew that. Here was the gun, but somebody else

45

had to be the trigger. Now she thought she knew the way.

Her lamp had been turned low on the dresser. She blew it out and slipped a cloak about her bare shoulders in the darkness and went quickly from the room, softly closing the door behind her.

When the time came for lamp-lighting, Larkin had stayed flat on his back on the bed in his room in the Amarillo House, his hands hooked at the back of his neck, his eyes fixed sightlessly on a stain in the ceiling overhead. He liked the darkness; it was soft and comforting and closed out the rest of the world, even though the rising roar of sound from Santone Street percolated through the thin planking of this hotel.

There was no self-pity in him, but only a sort of listlessness, induced, he supposed, by the rigours of a long and futile trail. He'd been told that Amy Pierce was now Amy Abbott, and that put an end to a page. In due time he would turn another page; life had always been like that. He only wondered now what was keeping him in Swayback. He had meant to come into town, take a room, make himself presentable, seek out Amy if she were in Swayback, do a bit of business with a justice of the peace, and ride on, with her at his side. If the girl were not in Swayback, he'd meant to stay until evening anyway, resting his horse and himself, and then he would have headed for Cultus Pierce's Boxed-C, and the ending would have been the same — a dream fulfilled. All that had been changed, yet he had waited until sundown anyway. All the sense had gone out of the pattern, yet he'd persisted in following it.

True, there was that hearing in justice court to-night, but already he'd decided not to be present. Before he'd parted with Matt Hobbs, he had told the old man all he had seen from the window of this room. Hobbs had his evidence for what it was worth. The only thing, then, to hold Larkin was that soft suggestion of Nick Diamond's that he be on his way. He had bridled at that suggestion had Larkin; he had taken it as a challenge and made his say, but now he could laugh at himself. You mixed in the little quarrels of little men and you gathered scars on your skin, and damned little else, for your trouble. You formed a habit of choosing sides, and it was hard to break. But that was another page of his life that was already put behind him, and it made no sense to turn backwards.

With that thought, though, he got to the core of his own indecisiveness; he had made his plans and his plans had gone awry, and there was no trail ahead for him. A man rode towards something, a distant hill, a distant dream, and when the thing proved to be a mirage, he had to find a new landmark for

48

himself. That was it. He had to get his bearings again, he had to fashion a new desire from the wreckage of the old; and that made his next step plain enough, for whatever he sought, it was not to be found in Swayback. Yet still he lay upon the bed, staring at that stain in the ceiling and wondering what kept him here.

Someone knocked on the door then — a soft, timorous tapping of knuckles, and the sound brought him to quick alertness. Swinging his feet to the floor, he slid them into his boots and sent a thoughtful glance at his warsack where he'd put his guns. But even then he sensed that there was no need for them. A man of authority rapped with authority; a man bent upon stealth did no announcing at all. Whoever was beyond that door had come with fear and misgivings. Yet when Larkin crossed the room to turn the key and swing the door open, he did so with a curious sidestepping movement that gave him a margin of safety if the greeting were to be couched in gun-smoke.

She stood out there in the dimness of the hall, tall and erect beneath a dark cloak that came to her chin, and it was the perfume she wore, faint and subtle and fraught with memories, that brought recognition to Larkin. She said, "Won't you ask me inside, Dave?"

His gesture gave her answer; she came into the room with a quick, gliding way she had of walking, and she closed the door and put her back to it. There was still light enough for him to see her, but, because he could find no other words, he said, "Just a moment and I'll light the lamp, Amy."

"No need," she said so urgently that it told him a lot. A sudden concern for her prompted him to say, "Anybody see you come here? Santone Street isn't what it used to be."

She said, "I came up the stairway to the back of the building. Before that I'd had a friend find out which room you were using. It took a little time and trouble."

He'd thought there was no bitterness in him, yet it put an edge to his voice. "The mayor's wife would have plenty of friends."

"I've hurt you, Dave," she said. "I can see that now. I thought perhaps that you'd changed so much that it wouldn't make any difference. But you were going to ride out of town without even looking me up to say hallo and good-bye. Do I really deserve that, Dave?"

He said simply, "I thought you'd wait, Amy."

"But you never wrote," she protested. "Not after the first six months or so. It's been seven years, Dave. And then I was told that you were dead — killed in a gunfight down in Dodge City."

He said, "I never had the time for writing, and I never was much of a hand at it anyway. I always figgered that you and me knew how we felt about things, Amy; we didn't need to remind ourselves every few weeks. But I wasn't killed in that Dodge City ruckus; you know that now. I laid in a bed for six weeks after trying to teach a bunch of wild Texican trail drovers that they had to check their guns when they hit Front Street. I wrote you then and told you I'd save the stake that we needed, and that I was coming home."

Her eyes lowered. "I know. I got that letter the day after I'd married Sheldon."

"Old Cultus is likely pleased," he said. "He got the kind of son-in-law he thought his daughter ought to be tied to. A steady, dependable fellow with the proper bankroll."

"I'm not so sure. Dad didn't dislike you, Dave, even though he ran you off the ranch because he discovered we were doing a lot of moonlight riding. I was all he had, Dave. He didn't want me tied to a common cowpoke. But he's mighty proud of the things he's heard about you since."

"And Abbott? You love him?"

"I don't know, Dave," she cried, and there was the ring of truth in it. "He was in love with me when you were still here. That's why he told you to stay away from me. And of course he's never forgiven you for ducking him in a horse trough that day you had words over me. After you left the range, he stayed away from me for a long time. Then he began riding out to the ranch for Sunday dinners. He took me to a dance or two. And he's the one who fetched me word that you'd been killed in Dodge. He asked me to marry him and we set a date then. You've got to understand me, Dave; I didn't know who to turn to, I was frightened and bewildered and lost. Even then I might not have gone through with it. But, a week before the wedding, he was thrown by a horse and trampled. It did something to his spine, put him in a wheel-chair. He's been getting better ever since, but it will be some time yet before he'll walk. He insisted that we go through with the wedding anyway, and I couldn't back out then. You wouldn't have wanted me to, Dave, if you'd been there to say. That's how I reasoned. He needed me, so I kept my word and married him."

"But do you love him?" he persisted.

"I don't know," she said again. "It hasn't been like a real marriage. Not with him crippled as he is. I just don't know, Dave."

He turned thoughtful until he became conscious that the silence between them was growing awkward. He said, "Yes, Amy, you did the only thing you could have done. I understand that now. Thanks a heap for coming here to tell me." He thrust out his hand. "It will be what you wanted it to be — hallo and good-bye."

She said, "Oh, no! You can't go!"

The room had grown oppressively warm. She fumbled at the tie-string of her cloak and removed the garment and let it fall across the chair. She wore a dark dress, low-cut and sheathing her tightly; she had bought it for a dinner given in Sheldon Abbott's honour by certain town dignitaries after the wedding, and she'd taken delight in the arched eyebrows of staider ladies. Now, in the gathering darkness, the alabaster whiteness of her arms and breast glimmered; the sun had never seemed to touch her, even in the days when she'd ridden free and wild over Cultus Pierce's many acres. He looked at her and said, "But I can't stay."

"Swayback needs you," she protested. "Haven't you been in the town long enough to learn that?"

"I've seen things," he admitted. "I've seen the change that's come, and I've seen a kid chopped down to death because a couple of men knew so little of fear or concern that they'd grown careless with guns. And I've

53

seen Matt Hobbs turned too old for his job. Yes, I know what you mean."

"Hobbs has resigned, Dave. All he's waiting for is somebody to take his place — somebody big enough to bring the law to Santone Street. And now you're back — a professional town-tamer, a man they speak of in the same breath with Wyatt Earp and Bat Masterson and Mysterious Dave Mather. Your reputation alone will be enough to put fear where it's needed."

He said, "I left Swayback to go out and make a name, to turn myself into the kind of a man that Cultus Pierce would be proud to have for a son-in-law. I even told your dad that, that last day, but it was a wild kid talking. I drifted south, and I became a deputy marshal in a Kansas town almost by accident. It was big money, bigger than I'd ever known, and sometimes when a man went down in the dust, it turned out that there was a price on his head. I earned more in some weeks than I'd earned in all my life here, and I told myself that even if the money was tainted with blood it was good money because it was my pay for bringing the only kind of law that would work on a frontier. But I had a goal in sight — a big enough stake to come back here and buy a piece of land and a few cattle and a house for you and me. It was a happy day when I reached that goal. I put my guns in my war-sack then, and they've stayed there since."

She said, "Is that dream gone beyond reclaiming? Oh, Dave, what are we to do?"

She swayed towards him; he saw the whiteness of her again, and the dark shadow that divided her breasts, and he knew that he had only to open his arms and she would be in them, soft and yielding, reluctant but surrendering, because he could beat down that reluctance by virtue of all that had once been between them. He didn't think then of honour, or of the solemnity of certain vows; he only knew that the page had been turned and there could be no turning back. He said, "We'd better be leaving here, Amy. It wouldn't do if someone should knock at that door."

She took the cloak from the chair and with a slow, dragging motion draped it about her shoulders. He fished coins from his pocket and placed the price of this room upon the bureau, then hoisted his war-sack to his shoulder and clapped his sombrero upon his head. She said then, listlessly, "There's no keeping you?"

"I'll ride this way again some time, Amy. I'll always want to know that you're getting along."

She said, "I know you, Dave. Once I knew you better than you knew yourself. There had to be something about you that made me single you out from all the others who rode for my father. There is something of the cavalier about you, something that makes you take on the troubles of weaker people. It drove you to the kind of work you did after you left here; it made you the kind of name you now own. You can't run away from this, Dave."

He laughed. "The shining knight on the great white horse, Amy? I thought so, once. I was younger then. But a bit of me died with every man who died beneath my guns. And they don't stay buried, those men; they parade through my sleep. Those who have bunked with me say that I fight a dozen fights all over again each night. To-day a man defied me to stay here. It was the worst thing he might have done; I almost accepted the challenge. But I remembered in time that I was through and done with that. No, Amy, I'm no cavalier come riding out of the cactus to play at being noble. But you'll never understand."

He let her into the hall, and they went walking towards the covered stairway at the rear of the building. A drunk came lurching up the steps from the lobby; instinctively Amy squeezed against the wall, but Larkin urged her onwards with the pressure of his free hand against her elbow. They groped their way down the thick and suffocating blackness of the rear stairway; they found themselves in the soft dusk of an alley.

"Let me see you home," he said.

"No, Dave, I'll make it from here," she countered. She turned silent then; each of them was mute with the consciousness that all had been said that could be said. She extended her hand. "Good-bye, Dave," she said. "Good luck to you. Remember me kindly — if you can."

He felt the firmness of her hand and was glad there was no trembling, and that there'd been no tears and would be none. He watched until her cloak made her one with the shadows, and she was gone. He moved on then, aimlessly at first, not wishing to think, nor daring to think; he remembered that it had been this way with a bullet wound; first there was the wooden numbness and then the pain followed. Recalled to reality, he bent his steps towards the livery stable that housed his horse. He had asked the hotel clerk about the place this afternoon, and after he'd eaten he'd gone to see what sort of care the animal was getting. He came in through the rear door of the stable and found a dim lantern burning, but the hostler was not upon his stool. When he reached the stall where his mount was standing, the girl in the cloak stepped forward.

For a wild and senseless moment he thought

it was Amy again — the cloak was of the same dark texture — but this girl had golden hair and her perfume was stronger. She said, "You're Dave Larkin? I was told that this was your horse."

He smiled. "You're spelling the hostler?"

"He's gone out to supper. I — I've been waiting here." Whatever it was she wanted to say, it was coming hard for her; he could see that. He said softly, "What is there I can do for you?"

One hand came from beneath the cloak and in it was a deck of playing-cards. She said, "Look at these cards, please. Look at the backs of them."

A frown of bewilderment wedging between his eyebrows, he took the cards in his hands and bent near the lantern and fanned them out. His examination was quick and thorough; he had known the gambling casinos of many towns, and most of the tricks of the tinhorn's trade. He said, "Where did you get these?"

"From a table in the Fandango." Her words came quick and breathless. "This is the deck that was being used when Banjo Sorenson charged the house-man with cheating this afternoon. I picked it up during the excitement. The deck is complete except for the hand that was dealt to Sorenson. He kept hold of it as he was thrown out."

Larkin whistled softly. "Better take these to Matt Hobbs."

She shook her head. "Nick Diamond will have the court buffaloed to-night. Hobbs will be afraid to make proper use of these. There was talk that you'd be at the hearing, Mr. Larkin. I was hoping *you*'d take them there."

He gave her a quick, sharp look. Her cloak had fallen open, and he saw the spangled dress beneath it; he thought he had her catalogued then, but he wasn't sure. There was that sweetness of face that gave the lie to his suspicion. "You want Banjo Sorenson out of jail, I take it," he said.

"The law will have to know whether Banjo was justified in starting a ruckus this afternoon," she explained. "If he was, then whatever happened was the fault of the Fandango men. But if he wasn't, then Banjo's morally to blame for the gun-slinging. You can see what a difference the cards will make."

"This Banjo? What's he to you?"

"Nothing. Or you might say a friend. He's new to the town. He's come to the Fandango a few times lately, a strange, sullen boy with something eating out his heart. I've seen that. I sing there. Once he asked me if I knew a certain song of the shantymen; he's from the Great Lakes country. I'd never been there, but I knew the song. I sang it for him. He

59

sat there wooden-faced, but he listened. He listened with everything that was in him. Now, whenever he comes in, I sing that song for him. He always thanks me. That's all."

But it was enough. Larkin saw it now, a respect grown in a girl's heart because it was something alien, yet something clean and bright in her world. He knew how she felt about this man; he knew it poignantly well. Yet: "I was set to ride out," he said. "It's none of my affair."

"No," she said, and her gaze met his and held it. "And it's none of mine either. But do you know what Nick Diamond would do to me if he suspected I'd taken those cards from the table?"

Larkin smiled. It was his first genuine smile since he'd sat his saddle and looked down upon Swayback from the ridge beneath the nooning sun. He said, "You'd better get back to the Fandango. You might be missed. I'll keep the cards, girl."

There was distance enough between Santone
Street and the town hall to the north of the
tracks for a man to reflect that most of the
things that happened to him came through his
own foolishness. Larkin, threading the bois-
terous street and coming past a railroad siding
where empty box-cars stood in angular silhouette against the darkling sky, paused in
the shadow of a dripping water tank and
shaped up a cigarette, cupping the match
quickly and letting little of the light show. This
was old habit; he was unconscious of his own
wariness. He had left his horse at the livery
stable, and also his war-sack. Thus, in a sense,
he had made a choice, yet the bridge wasn't
burned behind him.

A slight tremor had taken hold of him; he
was using the weed to quiet himself; and he
knew this feeling for what it was — anticipation. It put a tingle in his fingers, and it
had quickened his footsteps. He wondered
then if he had fashioned himself into something that couldn't be changed — if it was
his lot to always trouble himself with the little
quarrels of little men. He made his silent vow
that another hour would find him out of Sway-

back; he drew a measure of surety from this decision, and, stamping out the cigarette, he swung on northwards.

The justice court of Joshua X. Bragg was lamp-lighted when he found his way into it; the yellowness softened the harsh outlines of benches and chairs and the dusty drabness of the room. Sorenson was here, sitting stolidly to the front, his china-blue eyes solemnly considering his boot-toes. Nick Diamond was here, too, and Sig Kinsella was with him, the two from the Fandango ranged along one wall, before the biggest window, their backs to the sill, their arms folded. Another pair sat to the rear of the room, a man and a woman, shoulder to shoulder and silent with grief. It was Larkin's guess that these were the parents of the Davis boy who'd died in Santone's dust. Judge Bragg was behind his desk, and Matt Hobbs was holding a whispered consultation with him. Only these seven were in the room.

This surprised Larkin; in a sense two factions were opposed to-night; two halves of a town, and that made the hearing vital to all the citizenry of Swayback. Curiosity should have drawn many, if concern alone failed to motivate them. Yet Swayback had stayed at home. Then Larkin understood. The people of Santone Street hadn't come because Nick Diamond was here to handle his own affair, and Diamond needed no backing other than Kinsella. And the people from the north of the tracks were home because they hadn't heard of this. Matt Hobbs had scheduled the hearing, and Matt Hobbs hadn't advertised the affair. A man was chary of calling upon others to witness his own abasement.

That was it, and Larkin knew neither contempt nor pity for Swayback's law, but a certain sorrow instead. But he fought off this feeling; he had succumbed to it once to-night when the girl, Melody, had accosted him in the livery stable. He came up the aisle; he had a quiet way of walking, and he was almost to the front before he was discovered He said, "Evening, Matt. I'm here as a witness. Where do I sit?"

Hobbs' eyes lighted, the light was made of more than surprise and delight; there was hope in Hobbs, and Larkin wished it weren't there, for the hope reached beyond this room and this night, and that made it unfounded. Sorenson lifted his glance to Larkin, showing no sign of feeling; Kinsella frowned; Nick Diamond smiled. Of them all, only Joshua Bragg made a real show. He came ponderously to his feet, thrust forth a pudgy hand and said, "Welcome, suh! You, I presume, are the famous Dave Larkin. Hobbs heah, has told me that you served as a deputy under my late lamented friend, Wild Bill Hickok. I, suh, was at Wild Bill's elbow that day before the Bird-Cage dance hall in Dodge City when Hickok killed those two cowboys, Walker and Wagner. Mighty pretty shooting it was, suh."

Larkin came through the opening in the low railing that separated Bragg's desk from the rest of the room; he took Bragg's extended hand, but he said, "Aren't you a little mixed up, Judge? It was Bat Masterson who did the shooting you mentioned. He was avenging the death of his brother, Ed Masterson, who was killed by Wagner."

Bragg coloured, tugged at his skimpy goatee and finally hid his confusion behind a large bandanna by vigorously blowing his nose. "Your pardon, suh," he said. "An old man's memory . . ."

Diamond, from the far wall, shifted impatiently and said, "This is my busy night, Judge. Can't you get this show started?"

Bragg's glance was almost grateful, then he donned official dignity as he might have donned a hat. "Very well, suh," he said, and turned to address Sorenson. "Prisoner, will you stand and face the co't. You've been accused of disturbing the peace without justification. Your name, suh, for the records."

Sorenson came to his feet, tossing a shock of his yellow hair from his eyes by a quick jerk of his head. "I ban *Yoe* Sorenson," he said. "I ban tired of trying to tell fellers my name."

"Banjo Sorenson," Bragg said. "Put that down, will you, Matt? Now Banjo, theah is evidence that you, suh, disturbed the tranquillity of Santone Street by goading Sig Kinsella, heah, to gunplay. By the way, Mistah Diamond, where's that other employee of yours who was in on the shooting?"

"He had a headache," Diamond said lazily. "He didn't feel like coming."

Bragg coloured again and swiftly reverted his attention to Sorenson. "It seems, suh, that you accused a Fandango house-man of cheating you at cards." The judge gestured towards his desk top upon which lay a battered pair of spurs and five playing-cards. Larkin remembered the spurs; that barefooted boy had been wearing them. Bragg picked up the cards. "This was the hand you held, suh. I've examined it. I'll admit that getting cards as poor as these would goad anybody to violence. But theah's nothing wrong with them otherwise, suh."

Sorenson said, "I ban thinking that too many good cards vas always going to other fellers."

Larkin stood leaning on the inside of the railing. He took cards from his pocket and tossed them to Bragg's desk. "Look these

65

over, Judge," he suggested. "It's the rest of the deck. You can satisfy yourself about that by checking. The cards Sorenson held are missing."

Bragg, patently puzzled, fanned out the cards, face up. His examination was swift, and he said, "By gad, suh, you're right! But —"

"Now turn them over," Larkin said. "Notice the scrollwork on the backs? It matches with the cards Sorenson had, I'll bet. But you'll find one difference. High cards are marked by a slight deviation from the design of the backs. You see, Sorenson was being cheated. The house knew exactly what kind of cards each player was getting."

Bragg said, "That's right, suh! Where did you get these cards?"

"They came from the Fandango."

Over by the window, Sig Kinsella had stiffened, then dropped into a half-crouch; Larkin saw that from the corner of his eye. Nick Diamond had moved too, but he'd only propped his elbow on the window-sill. An easy affability was in his smile, but the white of his teeth showed and that took the humour out of it. He said, "I didn't know you'd paid my place a visit since you came to Swayback, Mr. Larkin."

"This is no frame," Larkin said. "If those cards didn't come from your place, how can

66

you account for the fact that the very ones that are missing are the ones Sorenson kept in his fist when he was thrown out of the Fandango?"

Diamond shrugged; he was a man who knew when he was beaten, and he had the knack of surrendering gracefully; Larkin had to concede that. "I see I'll have to fire one of my house-men," Diamond said. "When I hire them, I tell them the rules of my place, but sometimes they're overly zealous. Judge, the joke's on me."

Bragg was like a man who'd watched helplessly while a fuse had crawled towards a powder keg, and his obvious relief was that the keg had proved to be full of sand. He cleared his throat and spoke loudly, but there was a quaver in his voice. "Then, suh," he said, "since you are the employer of the men who were in the wrong, I must fine you, suh. One thousand dollars and co't costs."

Diamond said, "That's a little steep, isn't it, Judge?"

"The co't costs, suh, are all I'll retain. The thousand dollars go to the bereaved parents of the boy who was the innocent bystander in this case. It will provide proper burial, suh, and some cash recompense for theah tremendous loss."

"I'd forgotten about the boy," Diamond

said. "Fair enough, Judge. I'll send over the money in the morning."

Thus had the hearing come to its abrupt end, and Matthew Hobbs had taken on stature during this last interplay; there was a new squareness to his shoulders, a new lift to his voice. He said exultantly, "Ye've gotten a sample, Diamond, of the kind of law Swayback's having from here on out. Ye're staying, Dave? Ye're taking over my badge?"

Diamond smiled. "The town marshal's job pays, I believe, one hundred a month, Mr. Larkin. I could use a man of your calibre in my place, merely to stand around and keep order. Would three hundred a month interest you? I've been told that the guns of your kind are for sale to the highest bidder."

Larkin vaulted the railing then. Afterwards he was to try and analyse just what prompted the tremendous anger that boiled up in him at Diamond's offer; at the moment he only recognised it as an insult not only to himself but to Swayback's law. But there was more to it than that; there was the hate of one breed of man for another, and all the frustration and irony of this day was somehow mixed into it. He came charging at Diamond, sweeping chairs out of the way, and Diamond had time only to get his hand under his coat and to the gun that bulged there. Larkin struck the man's hand away, and a tiny derringer clattered to the floor. Then Larkin got one hand on Diamond's throat and the other at his crotch, and he lifted Diamond and hurled him bodily through the window, carrying the glass and part of the sash away.

Larkin remembered his danger then, but above the explosion of sound he heard the voice of Matt Hobbs, high and shrill. "Steady, Kinsella!" the marshal was shouting. "Steady, now!"

Hobbs had a gun in his hand, and Kinsella stood with his fingers spread and stiffened above the gun at his thigh, frozen in this crouching stance of a professional gunman by Hobbs' weapon. Sorenson's china-blue eyes had widened; Judge Bragg was held rigid, and even the man and woman to the back of the room were jarred out of their grief. Larkin, panting, spun upon Kinsella.

"Get outside and drag him back to where he belongs," he said. "Do you hear me? Take him south of the tracks and tell him to stay over there. Now get at it!"

The stiffness went out of Kinsella, but he was careful to keep his hand away from his holster. He spat contemptuously and took a moment to measure Larkin from head to foot, and hate was in his eyes. He said, "This is your hand, mister, and you've got friends to back you. But you'll live to be sorry for this."

Brushing away some of the broken shards of glass that still clung to the window-sash, Kinsella hoisted himself out of the room and was gone into the darkness. They could hear him helping Diamond to his feet; there were some mumbled words between the two, and then they went stumbling away. Bragg expelled a gusty sigh and looked upon Larkin fondly. "I can see, suh, that your reputation has a good foundation in fact."

Hobbs said, "It made a mighty nice show, Dave. A mighty nice show. The talk of this will sweep the town before midnight. Ye *are* staying, eh, Dave?"

Larkin said, "No, Matt. You've got to understand that — all of you. I've stayed too long now." The aftermath of exertion and excitement was upon him. He felt tired and burned out and a little disgusted with himself, not for what he'd done but because he'd let his anger run away with him.

Sorenson came to Larkin's elbow, fumbled for words and said, "I ban thank you," as simply as that.

Larkin put his hand on the giant's shoulder and said, "That's all right, feller. That's all right."

Then he felt Sorenson stiffening beneath his touch, and it came to him that here was a man of tremendous physical power, but even then he didn't understand what was electrifying the fellow. Sorenson's gaze was riveted upon the desk top beyond the railing, and Sorenson clambered over the railing and reached the desk and swept up the pair of spurs that lay there. They were big spurs; the rowels were designed for cruelty, but three of the tines had been broken from one of the wheels. Sorenson turned them over in his hand and said hoarsely, "Whose are these, Judge?"

"The kid's," Bragg said. "The Davis boy who was killed. He was wearing them. The undertaker fetched them here, not knowing what else to do with them, suh."

Sorenson said, "The man! That feller who come to my shack and killed Greta. His spur got broke in big fight in shack, see! I ban looking all over Swayback for spurs with three missing parts to wheel!"

Turning, he shouted the length of the room at the man and woman who were heading towards the door. "These spurs? Where your boy get them?"

The woman turned; she was small and pitifully frail, and grief had marked her. She said listlessly, "I don't know. He came home with them a few days ago. Said he'd found them some place. I supposed they'd been thrown away because one was broken. He took to wearing them after that."

Judge Bragg had been frowning thoughtfully; now he said, "Look heah, Banjo. Don't you think you'd better leave this town, suh? The Diamond crew won't remember you kindly for the licking they took in this co't to-night."

"That's right," Matt Hobbs said hastily. "I can't order you out. Not now. But you'd be playing it smart to get on your way."

Sorenson's face had turned wooden, but his eyes were aflame. "I ban staying now," he said doggedly. "I ban staying to look *good*."

All of this was beyond Larkin's understanding; he'd seen Sorenson's vast astonishment at finding the spurs, and he sensed a great tragedy and a great hate, and a determination that had somehow been renewed by this incident. But these were matters that were not for him; he'd finished his business in Swayback, and, while the two officials turned their arguments upon the Swede, Larkin seized the opportunity to slip across to the broken window and climb through it. This was the way he wanted to go; any good-bye would be superfluous and he was in no mood to batter down further insistence that he stay in Swayback.

Still, some might say that he was running away now; there'd be talk that he'd attacked Nick Diamond and then fled town to escape the consequences. But he was not concerned. He had learned long ago that people put their own estimation upon a man's acts, and that estimation was coloured by whatever it suited them best to believe. Santone Street would find comfort in his departure; another section of the town would remember that he'd brought justice into Judge Bragg's court and emphasised it with his own brand of violence. Thus he had served Swayback, for he'd given an element of its citizenry something to hearten it, an example of how Nick Diamond's kind might be handled. That was the size of it. The page had been turned.

So thinking, he came again into the shadow of the water tank where he'd paused to smoke, and it was here that some instinct of his trade gave him sudden, electrifying warning. Perhaps a boot-sole had scraped in the darkness and he had heard it and identified the sound without being conscious of the process. Perhaps some other slight furtive movement had been communicated to him. He had that one quick moment to ready himself, and then the shadows were spawning forth a rush of men, a wave that beat against him and broke and engulfed him.

He felt the rocking force of fists. There were knuckles everywhere, and he tried to ward them off, but they were too many for him.

He struck out blindly, felt his fist connect with something solid, and a man grunted in pain. But a blow caught him behind one ear; lights danced before his eyes, and he went down to his knees. A man cursed exultantly, a boot crashed against Larkin's ribs, and then they were smothering him with their weight, flattening him to the ground, and fists were striking at him from everywhere.

He was hard put to cling to consciousness. He heard voices, but they blended to a roaring nothingness in his ears. Then the weight was removed from him, and he heard someone say, "If he isn't dead he's half-dead, and that's the way the boss wants him to go out of here. If it was my say-so, he'd be turned into buzzard bait, and no ifs about it."

That was Sig Kinsella who had spoken. It was Larkin's thought that Diamond's crowd had moved against him in reprisal mighty quickly, and he sensed here a ready organisation, trained in violence.

But now they were lifting him from the ground, carrying him; he tried to gauge the direction, but it was useless. They came to a pause and he heard a scraping sound and searched his mind trying to place it, but it wasn't until he was heaved to drop on to hard planking and the sound was repeated that he realised he'd been tossed into an empty box-car and the door closed after him.

For a while he merely lay still, fighting to regain his strength but knowing that it was a futile fight. He wondered if they'd cracked a rib, and he wasn't sure, even when he managed to get to his hands and knees. He stayed in this position for a long moment, shaking his head and trying to clear it before he attempted to rise to his feet. The car lurched violently, this and others coupled to it shuddering to a sudden shock, and he went sprawling again. He heard the hoarse voice of a train whistle, and he realised that an engine was snaking this string of empties out of the siding.

Desperation seized him then; he had intended to leave Swayback to-night, but not this way, beaten and tossed here to be toted aimlessly to some unknown destination, or perhaps to die from hurts that needed attending. He put all his strength into one gigantic effort to pull himself to his knees again, but his muscles refused to obey him, and his head whirled with the effort.

He felt the train gathering speed; he heard the cry of the whistle once more, and the steady monotonous clacking of the wheels over the rails became a ceaseless refrain. This was in his ears when consciousness deserted him, and he lay motionless upon the floor of the car, no longer fighting, no longer caring.

Night's thin chill still had hold of the hills
when King Conover came out of his blankets
in the sunless dawn, and here in the cavern
that housed his outlaw brood the shadows lay
thick and heavy. Sleep's sluggishness made
Conover slow, but no motion of his was
wasted. He got into his boots and latched his
belt around him and punched some shape into
the sombrero that had served him as a pillow,
doing all these things in an habitual silence
that brought no stir from the mounded figures
of his men dotting the cave's hard floor.

Dressed, Conover came out of the cave to
stand on a wide, shelf-like ledge, the immensity of a perpendicular wall rearing skywards
at his back, while a wide and equally perpendicular gorge yawned before him. Across
this gorge sagged a suspension bridge, rope-
girded and crude of construction. The cavern
and ledge were nature's work; Conover had
made of these a natural fortress by driving
his men to the grumbling labour of building
the bridge. The human element of this scheme
of protection was represented this morning by
a man who sat huddled at the ledge end of
the bridge, a blanket about his shoulders, a

rifle cradled across his lap. His bearded chin was on his chest, his sombrero had slid down to the bridge of his nose, and he was fast asleep.

Conover looked at him with an impersonal sort of scorn, crossed over and nudged the guard not ungently with the toe of his boot. "Better stir up a fire," Conover said as the other came suddenly awake. "Me, I'm taking a little *pasear*."

He went across the bridge then, stepping in a queer, sideways fashion to accommodate his big body to the sway of the span, and keeping his eyes away from the tiny thread of a creek that brawled far below, at the gorge's rocky bottom. The far wall reached, his footsteps took him into crowded timber, a thick stand of lodgepole pine, and to a small corral that had been barely visible from the ledge. Here he found a lariat, snaked out his own horse, saddled it and went silently riding on through the timber.

His big stomach reminded him that he'd not eaten since nightfall, but there was another need within him, too, and it had sent him on this solitary trail. He recognised it now as a desire to be alone, to do some thinking away from the constant bickering and eternal poker-playing of his men. He had a crew that was the terror of the rangeland spreading below these foothills; they had moved much prime beef in the dark of the moon; they had given a nervous wariness to stage-coach drivers who threaded the land; and they were well fitted for all such work. But between forays they grew morose and irritable. That was the way of the owl-hoot, of the dim trails beyond the law; there were those wild, reckless moments when the blood surged hotly and danger rode the wind, but between these high-living moments was a monotony and boredom that gnawed at men's nerves.

A month of such inactivity had taken its toll. A month before there'd been the last raid, a wild foray to the flats that had been aimed at Cultus Pierce's sleek Boxed-C cattle and had culminated in gun-smoke and a desperate retreat. Crad Conover had been missing when heads were counted in the safety of tall timber, and Crad Conover had since been hauled to Swayback's jail by Cultus Pierce and lodged there pending trial on a charge of rustling. Since then, all of King Conover's scheming and all of his waiting had been directed to one end. They hanged men for cattle-rustling in Montana; and a Conover might die violently, but no Conover had ever kicked out his life at the end of a rope. Yet to snatch a man from Swayback's jail would be no mean feat; it would take quiet calculation and reckless daring, and the sign had to be right when the hour struck.

Thus, within big King Conover, salty old he-wolf of the hills, an habitual wariness and a wild impatience made constant war. Never gregarious, a man given to fighting his own battles in his own way, he had awakened with a vague need to shed himself of his men for the day. Now he picked his way along a ghost of a trail that bent in quick curves and dropped him always downwards until at last he came out upon a high promontory that gave him a sweeping view of the flat country stretching to the limitless east.

Here he sat his saddle, angling one sinewy leg around the horn, twisting a cigarette into shape and viewing the panorama below through its thin smoke. The sun stood above the eastern horizon, the flats lay mellow and tawny and sagebrush shadowed beneath this first light. Not far distant, smoke spiralled from the group of buildings that was Boxed-C's headquarters; beyond and clearly etched at this hour was Swayback. Conover's eyes dwelt on the town and did their dreaming. That was the enemy, that distant scatteration of buildings; that was the redoubt he must storm if Crad Conover was to be free.

He had been a soldier once, had Conover, and it had taught him to think in such terms.

He had followed Dixie's ill-fated flag to the finish, yet his soldiering had not been the disciplined war-making of the men who looked to such as Lee for leadership. The black flag of Quantrell had been King Conover's banner; he had been with that blue-eyed guerrilla leader when the streets of Lawrence, Kansas, had been strewn with dead men; he had had such men as Frank and Jesse James for brothers-in-arms. These had been his companions; this had been his school.

Under such tutorship Conover had learned to handle a six-shooter and to ride, and he'd brought these skills with him out of the strife — these and a restlessness that would be with him always. That restlessness had taken him on a far trail and fashioned him into what he was. It had coloured his personality and altered his way of thinking. Other men had come out of the war to take up old paths again, to help heal a broken nation; they had won to positions of trust and respectability. King Conover was not one of these; his star had been as dark and restless as himself.

Now the shadow of him had fallen over this stretch of Montana, and that shadow had, in a different way, touched young Crad Conover. There was in Crad a hero-worship for this wildling older brother whose name had already become something of a legend. His worship had shown itself in an unconscious aping of King Conover's mannerisms and a studied determination on Crad's part to excel in any raid they undertook. This recklessness had been Crad's undoing in the last foray. And because King Conover sensed these things, he also recognised the only responsibility he had ever willingly accepted. Crad Conover had gotten into trouble, and King Conover must get him out of it.

Yet even with this thought in him, King's mind turned to more material matters as he studied Swayback in the morning's clearness. A man stayed true to his blood, but a man kept his eye open for other things too. There was a bank in Swayback, its vault bulging with the deposits of ranchers, and the money left by cattle-buyers who might want quick and ready cash within reach. That bank had occupied Conover's thoughts before. Sometimes a fellow could kill two birds with one stone. . . .

He turned away from the promontory after a half-hour of thoughtful scrutiny; the demands of his stomach were drawing him back to the cavern hideout of his men, yet he took a circuitous route. It behoved him to keep an eye on the hills that sheltered him, and that sleeping sentry at the cave end of the bridge this morning had been just another indication that a man could not pin too much of his trust in others. He moved on through the timber, hearing all of the waking voices of the woodlands, smelling the everlasting aroma of the pines, and he came in this manner to the railroad tracks that climbed up into the hills.

For a while he chose to parallel these tracks, but not too closely; he kept away from the embankment, screening himself always behind the trees, and he rode this way until he neared a water tank that perched upon spindly legs beside the track. And here it was that he saw the man sprawled beside the embankment.

The fellow lay face down and motionless, and at first glance Conover thought that he was a dead one. Tugging gently on the reins, Conover brought his horse to a stand, and for a long moment the outlaw was as silent and unmoving as the sprawled figure. Then Conover came down from the saddle with care and moved with equal care, not towards the figure but in a wide circle around it.

His eyes were busy all the while, and the things Conover saw, and the things he expected to see and didn't, all painted for him a complete and telling picture. This man had come here neither afoot nor ahorse; therefore it followed that the freight train which had passed through the hills the night before had brought him. The train had stopped at the water tank; the man had either climbed from it or been thrown from it then. And the man had not had the strength to crawl more than a few yards afterwards.

These things established in Conover's mind, the big outlaw came towards the fallen man; he had already noticed that the fellow wore no guns; now he saw that the man had been badly used. He turned the man over, felt of the heart and found it beating, and he studied the dirt-smeared, bruised face for a long time. Then he began rifling the pockets. There was a wallet containing papers, and when Conover had examined these, he knew that the man was Dave Larkin.

Whereupon King Conover withdrew to a rock a few feet distant, seated himself and spun another cigarette and sought to draw wisdom from the weed. Conover had ranged these hills in the days when a younger Dave Larkin had ridden for the Boxed-C, but the outlaw had never known Larkin, and it had taken the papers to establish the identity. Larkin as a legend in later years, he had known, of course; the tales of towns tamed had seeped up to Swayback and into the hills beyond. And the news of Larkin's return had been fetched to the hideout yesterday. It had interested Conover to no great degree then, but the finding of Larkin here unconscious to-day had suggested vague potentialities on Conover's mind. His thoughts had to do with an affinity he had found to exist among all men who wore the law's tin; he shaped this into something concrete as the tobacco burned.

In due course he stamped out the cigarette and came again to Larkin, getting an arm under the unconscious man and hoisting Larkin to his shoulder. The weight of Larkin bowed the outlaw — there was solid poundage in that lean body — and he went staggering to the horse and draped the unconscious form over the animal, behind the saddle. The horse shied and threatened to buck off this burden; Conover put a soothing hand upon the mount, and spoke soft and reassuring words. Then he took his lariat and lashed Larkin in place.

Into the saddle again, Conover sought out a trail and began climbing it, bending sometimes to avoid the slap of low-sweeping branches. He came slowly; the horse was double-burdened and the ascent was steep, and it was nearly noon when Conover reached the hidden corral on the near side of the gorge. But by then the outlaw had forgotten his hunger; he was a man possessed of a vast idea, and it filled him to the exclusion of all else.

The horse turned into the corral and, un-saddled, Conover loosened the knots that held

Larkin and found Larkin still unconscious. Again Conover draped his burden over his shoulder. He managed very well until he reached the suspension bridge, but here he had to use his free hand on the rope railing, and there was no way to counteract the sway of the bridge. On the far ledge his men had spied him and were collecting in a knot, calling to each other and gesticulating. Conover shouted, "Some of you fools come out here and give me a hand!"

A couple of them moved to help; they got Larkin by the shoulders and legs and edged along the bridge with him. When they reached the ledge, Conover saw then that someone was here who hadn't been here when he'd left, and to this lean and wiry newcomer Conover said, "Either you got up early or you rode mighty hard, if you came from Swayback this morning."

"Both," said Sig Kinsella and turned his gaze upon Larkin, who had been dumped upon the ledge. The first surprise at recognising Conover's burden was gone from Kinsella and annoyance had taken its place. "Where did you run across him?"

"By the water tank," Conover said with a sweeping gesture. "He'd been dumped off the freight from the way the sign read. He's Dave Larkin."

"I know that!" Kinsella snapped. "He rubbed Nick Diamond the wrong way last evening, so we roughed him up and loaded him on the freight. Nick won't thank you for this, King."

"I wasn't thinking about Nick," Conover rumbled. "I was thinking about Crad. I'm playing this town-tamer as I'd play a sleeve ace. Swapping a man for a man. Dave Larkin for Crad." Kinsella showed no enthusiasm. "Do you think for a minute that Matt Hobbs would listen to any such deal?"

"He'll listen — or Larkin's a gone gosling!"

Kinsella plucked his gun from its holster, and he said, "I was all for killing this customer last night. Nick wanted the job handled otherwise. Larkin's something of a hero in Swayback; if we'd done for him and left him laying, we might have got the whole town aroused against us. Or so Nick said. Nick argued that beating him up and shipping him out of town would be a way of getting rid of him that would stick. Larkin wouldn't come back for more of the same. But what held true in Swayback don't hold true here. Step aside, Conover!"

Kinsella's gun tilted downwards, and Conover said, "Plant a bullet in him, Sig, and you'll come walking into hell right on his heels! He stays alive."

Kinsella hesitated. "You'll want him dead yourself before another day. When he opens his eyes, he'll see this hideout. He might remember it."

"Never mind about that," Conover said and brushed all the arguing aside with a wave of his hand. "What fetched you here to-day, anyway?"

"Nick's found out all you need to know, King. He sent me to pass the word along to you. Charlie Peters, the cashier, opens the bank at eight in the morning. Old Abercrombie comes in between nine and ten, and goes home to eat between noon and one o'clock. When Abercrombie gets back, Peters goes out to put on the nose-bag — usually at the Chinaman's. Nick says to tell you he's had them timed for almost a month. Abercrombie gets to the bank in the morning whenever it pleases him, and sometimes he leaves early in the afternoon. But there's one thing you can set your watch by, according to Nick: Charlie Peters is alone there between twelve and one."

Conover fingered his jaw and said, "That's fine. There's less people on the street at the noon hour. But you can ride back and tell Nick that I'm not hitting the bank until I've tried this new scheme of getting Crad out of the calaboose. If this little trick doesn't take the hand, I'll do my bank-busting and jail-busting at the same time."

"You're crazy," Kinsella scoffed, but not with vehemence, though he still held his gun. "How you gonna make a deal with Matt Hobbs?"

"I done my thinking about that while I was climbing back up here," Conover said. "I'm counting on Nick Diamond to make the dicker; he can do it any way he wants. Here's Larkin's wallet; it's got papers that couldn't belong to anybody but Larkin. That should convince Hobbs that our dicker ain't bluff. The Boxed-C has an old north line shack they haven't used for a long time. Have Nick get word to Hobbs to have Crad at that line shack at midnight to-night. We'll be there with Larkin. And tell Hobbs that if he has a posse hidden off in the shadows, the first bullet I fire will be for him, and the second for Larkin."

Kinsella shook his head. "If Hobbs is loco enough to make the swap, that means Larkin will be back in Swayback, and it also means he'll be beholden enough to Hobbs that he'll likely take over the marshal's job for Hobbs. That ain't going to be to Nick's liking, King. I'm thinking you could do the same stroke of business with a dead Larkin as easy as you could with a live one."

He tilted the gun again, and Conover said, "Put that iron away, Sig!"

Still Kinsella kept the gun in his hand, and Conover said, "Get this straight, Sig. My deal with Diamond is a good deal; it means that he's found out all I need to know about that bank before hitting it, and Diamond will get his cut for doing the trick I'd have had trouble doing. Maybe we'll make other deals later on. But I'm the ramrod here in the hills. Now put down that gun!"

They stood thus, their eyes locked, the eagle of the hills and the weasel from Swayback's Santone Street, but something furtive came into Kinsella's glance and all of the arrogance went out of him. Casing the gun, he said, "I'm not fool enough to try bucking you and your whole crew, King. But you're making a mistake. Remember this — what's bad for Nick is bad for you, now. We're tied together from here on out. But there'll be a day — and soon, maybe — when you'll wish you'd let me make buzzard bait out of Larkin here and now."

A smile broke the stony bleakness of King Conover's face. "There's a time for guns — and a time for scheming," he said. "You'll learn that after you've put a few more years behind you, Kinsella. Right now I'm playing a scheme through, and the finish will come when Matt Hobbs turns Crad over to me at

Pierce's line shack at midnight. Tell Nick I'll be doing a little favour for him — then." He smiled a quick and crafty smile. "The first shot will be for Larkin — the second for Hobbs."

Kinsella smiled too. "I should have savvied, King," he said. "I'll be riding now."

Such was the talk that came to Dave Larkin as he lay where he'd been spilled upon the ledge. His eyes were still closed, but his ears were tuned to every sound; he interpreted these for what they meant, and he heard the beat of Sig Kinsella's boots as Diamond's man crossed the rocky ledge. The suspension bridge creaked, and Conover spoke again, saying, "Some of you boys drag Larkin into the cave. Better tie him up when you get him there. He should be coming alive soon, if he's going to."

Twice since unconsciousness had claimed him as the freight train had rolled out of Swayback the night before, Larkin had managed to command his faculties. The first time had been when the train had toiled to a brief stop at the mountain water tank; it was there that Larkin had succeeded in easing back the door of the box-car. But there'd been no strength left in him to clamber to the ground, so he'd rolled out instead, rolled to tumble down the embankment and back to unconsciousness.

That second long sleep had ended as he'd been taken from Conover's horse at the hidden corral. He had chosen then to maintain a pretence of unconciousness; this was another of those instincts of warier days; you didn't show your hand until you knew whether you faced a friend or an enemy. Now Larkin knew all he needed to know.

He felt someone tugging at his arm, and he let himself stay limp as he was dragged across the ledge and into the cave. His body was one vast ache; he still wasn't sure whether any of his bones had been broken, and he had to grit his teeth against pain as he was hauled along. He soon sensed that he was in some sort of an interior; the sun no longer blazed against his closed eyelids. He heard someone say, "Hustle over to the corral and get a rope, will you? You heard King say to tie him up."

This was the time when he must make his play, Larkin knew. There was in him no desire to stay here and play hostage for King Conover only to die when the game came to its finish at Pierce's line shack. Two lives would be in danger there — his own and Matt Hobbs'. Now only his own skin was in jeopardy, and Conover might be a little less quick to kill him now, since the outlaw needed a live Larkin to finish his negotiations with Hobbs. But if there was any chance of escaping, it must come before his wrists were bound. So thinking, Larkin opened his eyes and rolled over on his side and drew up his feet, wondering the while if he had strength enough to come to a stand.

The lamp-lighting time had come again to
Swayback, and Matthew Hobbs stood in the
doorway of Judge Bragg's office just as he had
at this same hour the evening before. This
similarity of time and surroundings, plus an
acute consciousness of a new problem, gave
Hobbs pause; he wondered if it was becoming
habit with him to look to Bragg for wisdom,
and there was in him some spark of indepen-
dence that made him regret this. But Bragg
had already spied him; the greeting was made
and exchanged; and Hobbs came limping up
the aisle to slump into the witness chair.

Nothing was changed here; Bragg sat tilted
back in his chair, his boots crossed on the
desk's top, his walking-stick placed before
him, and the room was vast and shadowy, and
big with emptiness. But there was that broken
window; it hadn't yet been replaced, and a
burlap sack hung limply over the opening and
moved restlessly to the fingering of a slight
breeze. That was the one difference that
twenty-four hours had made, and Hobbs, seeing it, reached his own decision.

"I, suh, have read the note," Bragg said by
way of an opening, and ceased from fingering

his skimpy goatee long enough to indicate a paper upon his desk. "Also, I have examined the wallet which accompanied the missive. Theah is no argument but what it belonged to Dave Larkin. You said, suh, that you found these things on your office desk?"

"Late this afternoon," Hobbs said. "I leave my office open while I'm out; just about anybody might have come in and left the note. I fetched it right over to ye."

"An interesting document, suh," Bragg said, swinging his feet to the floor and reaching for the note. "It purports to be from King Conover, but his untutored hand never penned these lines. Consider, suh, the scholarly fist — the simplicity of words, and the economy of them. It leaves little for the imagination. Dave Larkin is in Conover's hands. Larkin dies unless you have Crad Conover at the Boxed-C line shack at midnight. That, suh, is the sum of it."

Worry drew Hobbs' tufted eyebrows together. "King Conover didn't come into Swayback and put a note on my desk," he said. "He had somebody do that for him, and Conover's friend likely wrote the note. Have ye thought what that means? It bodes no good for us that Conover has a friend here in Swayback. And I'm doubting no part of the note. Dave Larkin's not been seen since he left this room last night. He's gone from Swayback, yet his horse and his war-sack still wait for him at the livery stable over on Santone Street. Was he snatched from the town by Conover last night?"

Bragg sighed. "So it would seem, suh. Po' fellow."

Hobbs glanced at the broken window; he wasn't conscious of the act, but he knew the thought that had prompted it. He said, "Ye can save your sighs, Judge. Dave Larkin will be free by midnight. I'm turning Crad Conover loose if King keeps his part of the bargain."

Bragg took this announcement in silence; he put a long moment on meditation before he said, "Crad Conover, suh, is the property of all Swayback town. Have you considered that you might be seriously overstepping your authority by making such an exchange?"

"I've thought of it," Hobbs said with a show of heat. "To hell with Swayback town!"

"But, suh! If King Conover successfully accomplishes this coup, no citizen of Swayback will ever be safe again. Let one of Conover's crew end up in our calaboose, and our rustling friend will have only to snatch the first person he sees and hold him as hostage. I argue, suh, that such a method will become habit-forming."

"Look, ye," Hobbs said. "Swayback owes something to Dave Larkin. It owes him for an example he gave this town last night that's already taken hold. More than one man has stopped me on the street to-day and said that it might be a good idea to cross the tracks and clean out Santone Street. Larkin's big toe is worth more than Crad Conover's whole carcass, savvy? If Swayback doesn't like what I do to-night, it can bellow to me about it."

"Larkin alive and free and indebted to you, suh, would indeed be more valuable than young Conover," Bragg said meditatively. "Have you thought what form Larkin's gratitude might take?"

"No," said Hobbs, "and ye're following the wrong trail, Judge. Larkin will ride out just as he said he would. I'm not concerned with that. I'm only thinking of keeping him alive."

"You're not consulting the mayor before you take this step, suh?"

Hobbs smiled wryly. "He wouldn't approve of my removing Conover from his cell without proper court action. But I'll risk Sheldon Abbott's wrath. Do ye think he'll take my badge away from me?"

Judge Joshua Bragg came to a stand, and there was about him a solemn gravity that was entirely genuine. He said, "You, suh, are a good man, Hobbs. If Swayback's law must be

96

held to an accounting for what you do to-night, suh, I'll be proud to share the blame. You'll have to hurry to reach Pierce's line shack by midnight. Good evening, suh. And good luck."

Startled, Hobbs saw this new depth to Bragg and found himself closer to the man than he'd ever been in their brief association. The surge of affection that rose in him was an embarrassment; he had no words to match the other's, no way of voicing his appreciation for Bragg's pledge of loyalty, and he only said, "Why, thank ye, Judge," and went limping down the aisle.

Out of the building, Hobbs went first to the nearest livery stable, and when he emerged from its gloomy depth he was leading a saddled horse. At the hitchrack before the jail building he got his own mount, and he led the two horses to the deeper shadows that banked beside the log and frame structure. Coming inside the building, he groped in the darkness of the little ante-room to the front and took down a slicker from a wall peg. This garment was known to all Swayback and the range beyond; it had come with Hobbs from Texas, and rain had washed it and sun had beaten it until it was chalky and colourless, but he never took a trail without it. The slicker donned, he went into the cell corridor, fitted a key into the door of Crad Conover's cell and swung the door wide.

Light from a smoky overhanging lamp glinted on a gun in Hobbs' left hand as Conover stepped forward, and Hobbs produced a pair of handcuffs with his right and snapped these on Conover's wrists. Conover looked down at the bracelets in astonishment; the whole procedure had a touch of sleight-of-hand to it, and he said, "What's the idea?"

"You and me are taking a *pasear*," Hobbs said. "Come along now."

He led Conover to the outer door of the building; Hobbs paused here, eyeing the street as furtively as though this were a jail-break, and, seeing no one, he brought his prisoner briskly down the steps and around the corner to where the horses waited. His gesture sent Conover up into a saddle; Hobbs looped the reins of Conover's horse around the horn and got hold of a lead rope. Conover, his face puckered in puzzlement, said, "Just what kind of a deal is this?"

"Never ye mind," Hobbs said as he swung to his own saddle; and he knew a fleeting moment of regret. He had served his badge long and faithfully; the pull of one kind of loyalty tugged insistently at another and gave him no peace. But he led the way down an alley thick with darkness, and Crad Conover followed after him, holding to a bewildered silence. . . .

For the girl Melody this, too, was like the evening before it; again she lay stretched upon her bed in the room adjoining Nick Diamond's office over the Fandango, and again she'd removed the wadding from the knothole in the wall and was listening intently to the talk between Diamond and Sig Kinsella in the room beyond.

She did this with no misgivings; she had had much evidence that events of some importance had transpired within the last twenty-four hours, and now she was irrevocably involved in them. The die had been cast for her when she'd accosted Dave Larkin in the Santone Street livery stable and pressed a deck of cards upon him. Since then she had kept at her listening post whenever possible, hoping thus to have all the sequel to her own daring.

Nick Diamond had come back to the Fandango last night with his left arm held awkwardly, his clothes torn and his face bloody. From the little stage where she sang, Melody had witnessed his return; she had seen Diamond surreptitiously helped in by Sig Kinsella and quickly hurried up the stairs to his office. After that Kinsella had departed again, but before he'd left he'd beckoned to half a dozen of Diamond's men and they had followed after him. Later that evening they'd all returned, straggling in in twos and threes and saying little to anybody.

A doctor had put in an appearance and gone to Diamond's office and stayed an inordinately long time, but when Melody got to her bed there was only silence in the office beyond. She had lain sleeplessly, wondering what had transpired at the justice court hearing; she had heard the swamper stacking chairs upon tables in the bar-room below; every sound of this vast building had reached her and been translated, and then she had found the sunlight at her window and the lamp still burning upon her dresser.

Sig Kinsella was gone riding when she arose; she had not seen Nick Diamond all through the day, but she'd heard Kinsella come into the office in mid-afternoon, and there'd been talk. From it she'd learned much, and, putting the fragments together, she knew that Diamond had been worsted at the hearing and that Banjo Sorenson had gone free and that Dave Larkin had hurled Diamond through the justice court's window. The part about Sorenson, at least, would have been good news to her, but it was instantly cancelled by the other things she'd heard. Larkin had been beaten into unconsciousness and loaded aboard a freight train, and Larkin had tumbled

100

from that train to be picked up by King Conover.

These were the things Kinsella and his boss had discussed that afternoon; there was much ado about what had transpired on the mountain ledge, and thus Melody had learned of the secret relationship between Santone Street and the high hills to the west. After that, Diamond's pen had scratched and Kinsella had departed again, and now Kinsella was back. His report was briefer this time; a note had been placed in Matt Hobbs' office, but up until now Hobbs was still in town and Crad Conover was still in his cell.

To Melody, this was one more item to add to the sum of her knowledge, and she knew now what she must do and how she must do it. Through helping her, Dave Larkin had incurred the enmity of Nick Diamond and gotten himself beaten and shipped out of town. That had been the first of the chain of circumstances that had placed Larkin in his present predicament — a prisoner of King Conover and doomed to die once his usefulness as a hostage ended. Melody's reasoning was simple and direct — she had done this thing to Dave Larkin, therefore she must help him.

She even had her plan half-formed, but she waited until Diamond and Kinsella had left the office before she made her first move; never before had she been so cautious of any sound she made, but now she grew panicky at the thought that they might be reminded of her nearness. The office empty, she quickly changed to a divided riding skirt, a plaid shirt, and boots; and her golden hair was tucked under the high crown of a sombrero when she came down the stairs to the Fandango's bar-room.

Nick Diamond stood leaning against the bar, his left arm in a black sling, and one cheek masked beneath a bandage. His eyes lighted when he saw her. The Fandango ran all seven days of the week, but it was understood that one evening was her own. Usually she took Mondays off; they were the nights when the trade was the lightest, but she had veered from this procedure on other occasions, so she merely said, "I didn't sleep well last night, and I'd likely give a poor performance. I think I shall go riding."

She wondered if her voice sounded natural; she was not adept at this sort of deception; and she also wondered if she should show any curiosity about the sling and bandage he wore. Her eyes must have told him something of what was in her mind, for Diamond showed his teeth in a ghost of a smile, and said, "Very well, Melody. I'm quite a sight, eh? But you should see the other fellow."

He had never shown her anything but courtesy and kindness, yet she hated him in that moment; she wanted to say that it had taken half a dozen of his men to wreck his vengeance for him, and she was afraid that that thought, too, might be naked in her eyes. She went quickly from the saloon and down the boardwalk towards the livery stable, elbowing among the men who drifted along to the various places of pleasure, hurrying and yet trying not to show her need for haste. And in this manner she came to a quieter section of the street where a group of small boys played in a splash of yellow that fell from a nearby window, and here among them, hunkering on his heels and talking, was Banjo Sorenson.

Something about the sight of him checked her stride; he was so much like one of those urchins himself, only bigger; there was a simplicity to him that was balm to her ruffled nerves, and his kind of strength would be a comfort rather than a menace. The thought came to her that if her business was what Nick Diamond supposed it to be to-night, she would like to ask this big Scandinavian to ride with her across a moonlit range. But that was before she heard what Sorenson was saying.

He had a pair of spurs in his hands, and

he was showing them to these boys. "You yust think good and hard," he urged them. "Maybe you can remember how Yimmy Davis come to get these spurs. Maybe he told one of you, huh? I got to find the feller who used to own 'em."

His tone betrayed him; she had no inkling of the tragedy that had sent him headlong to Swayback in futile search, but she'd sensed the driving hate that kept him here, and she guessed now that the spurs were bound up in that hate. She gasped, her hand going to her throat, and he heard her then and lifted his eyes. Coming to his feet, he clawed the sombrero off his tousled yellow mane, and he said awkwardly, "Goot evening." She tried to take her eyes off the spurs in his hand and succeeded with an effort. He said, "You ain't singing to-night?"

She shook her head, and he said, "I ban sorry. I like to hear you sing." But she was already hurrying away, hoping she had not wounded him by her brusqueness but desperately afraid to keep standing there with her eyes on those spurs. She was almost running when she bobbed into the livery stable, and she was glad that the hostler was again absent. Finding the horse she usually rented, she helped herself to gear, scrawled a note to the hostler, and a few minutes later she was picking her way across the tracks.

To the north lay an unfamiliar world; she had visited it only in her first days in Swayback, and now she had some trouble locating the big building that housed the town's officials, and when she finally came into its corridor she found most of the flanking doors shut, but lamplight splashed into the hall from one open doorway. She poked her head into the justice court to find Judge Bragg just clearing his desk for the night. She said, "Pardon me. I was looking for Marshal Hobbs."

Bragg hoisted his brows; an acknowledged judge of whisky and horseflesh, he also had an eye for beauty. "Hobbs, miss?" he said. "He's gone out of town on business. 'Pears he won't be back until mawning. Is there anything I can do for you?"

She hesitated; there were fabulous tales of this man's exploits, and she had heard them in the Fandango. Now she was tempted to trust him with her information, but, "Yes, you can do this for me," she said. "You can forget that I was here."

Then she was hurrying out of the building, her plan crashed about her, for it had been her intention to lay all of the truth before Matt Hobbs, to warn him that a bullet was all he would get in return for Crad Conover, and to beg him to take a posse into the Silver Belts

105

at once. But she'd come too late for that; Hobbs was already gone. And, realising this, she shaped a new plan and swung astride her horse to head for the house of Sheldon Abbott on the far outskirts.

Again she had trouble finding her destination; she had to ask twice of men she passed, but she reached the house and found it aglow with light. Pausing in the shadow of a huge cottonwood on the far side of the street, she swung to the ground and stood hesitantly, not knowing what to do next. And while she stood here, Amy Abbott came out to the porch, put her hands to the railing and leaned outwards, obviously drinking in the softness of the night.

Melody came across the street then. Just beyond the fringe of light, she said, "Mrs. Abbott — ?"

Amy's eyes quested the darkness. "Yes — ?"

"I'd like to speak to you. Out here."

She realised how queer her words must sound; she half-expected the other woman to scream, or to turn quickly away and dart inside. But Amy came down the steps and walked towards her, pausing less than a dozen feet away. "I've seen you before, I think," Amy decided. "Aren't you one of the girls from Santone Street."

There was in that recognition no haughtiness nor disdain but rather the frank curiosity of the woman of one world who had found the opportunity to look upon a woman of another world at such a short distance. And knowing how she must stand catalogued in Amy Abbott's mind, Melody felt the burn of blood in her cheeks, and a rising antagonism made of her own kind of pride.

"I'm here because of Dave Larkin," she said.

"Dave?" Amy repeated, and her interest had quickened; Melody could see that. "What about Dave?"

"He's in danger," Melody said, her words tumbling after each other. "He's being held, up in the Silver Belts, by King Conover, and he'll be killed before the night's over if somebody doesn't help him."

Amy said, "How do you know this, girl?"

"Never mind," Melody cried. "What matters is that it's true."

"Why didn't you take your information to Marshal Hobbs?"

"But you don't understand!" Melody protested. "Marshal Hobbs is gone — gone to take Crad Conover to exchange for Dave Larkin at your father's old north line shack. But King Conover won't make the exchange; once he's gotten Crad Conover free, he'll shoot Hobbs and Larkin!"

If Amy's indifference had been pretended, she dropped all pretence now. "What is it that I can do?" she demanded quickly.

"Ride to your father's ranch," Melody said. "Get him to take his crew and head into the hills. Maybe they can find Conover's hideout and snatch Larkin away before it's too late."

She didn't realise how naïve this sounded; she hadn't stopped to think that if Cultus Pierce could thus easily find the rustlers' hideout, the Boxed-C would have long since carried a war of extermination to the high hills. But her excitement and desperate urgency had communicated itself to Amy now, for Amy took no time to challenge this flaw in Melody's scheming. But Amy was a woman still, and there was this one last unanswered question in her, and Melody, studying her in the half-light for her every reaction, saw it on Amy's lips.

"What brought you to *me?*" Amy asked. "What made you think I'd help?"

"I've learned a little about Dave Larkin since he came back to town," Melody said. "I've heard talk about him in — in the place where I work. It has been said that he was in love with you before he left here — and you with him. Also, I've seen Larkin. I don't know much about love, but I do know that a woman who once cared for him would always care for him. That's why I thought you'd help."

Amy said thoughtfully, "So you saw him. And now you're half wild with fear because he's in danger. Did it happen that quickly with you?"

Melody said stiffly, "We're not here to talk about me, Mrs. Abbott."

They had come together as aliens, these two, a woman who walked with respectability, and a woman who wore the taint of a dozen honkytonks. They stood now as enemies; a consciousness of this was alive in both of them, and yet at the very moment that the swords were unsheathed, they were both acutely aware of the need of another, and this made a truce between them. Amy said, "I'll ride out to my father's. Right away."

"You'd better hurry," Melody said, and faded back into the deeper shadows to where her horse waited beneath the cottonwood. From here she could see Amy hurrying back into the big house; the very fleetness of the other woman's footsteps proclaimed the wild need that was driving Amy now. Thus Melody might have gone about her own affairs; she had done all that could be done, she had made of Amy Abbott the instrument of action that would help Dave Larkin if help could come to him. But the responsibility could not be transferred so easily.

That was why Melody headed her horse out of Swayback, pointing the mount towards the distant lift of the Silver Belts and jogging the animal to a wild gallop.

To Dave Larkin, gathering himself to get to his feet in the cavern hideout of King Conover, there had come this calculated moment when it was now or never. Of the two men who had dragged him inside, one had gone to fetch a rope, the other stood waiting, his legs within reach of Larkin, his eyes turned towards the cave's wide mouth. Thus for an unguarded instant, the odds stood in Larkin's favour. These things he recognised as he planned his play: the need for silence, and for quick and ruthless action. His real fear was that his bruised body would not obey him. He would want a ready response of muscles, a surety of coordination in the next few minutes.

His knees drawn up, he put the heel of his right hand to the rocky floor, and, in so doing, he felt the roughness of a loose rock. It was the size of a hen's egg, and his fingers closed around it, and he rolled slightly then, putting the full weight of his body on his right hip. Lifting himself, he lurched to a quick stand; the slight sound brought Conover's man wheeling about, but there was less than a yard between them, and Larkin struck out with the rock, his blow catching the man beneath the left ear. The fellow's eyes rolled upward until only the whites showed; his knees began buckling, and Larkin caught him and lowered him gently and silently to the floor.

This exertion had put a trembling in Larkin; he stood swaying, afraid that he was going to fall across the sprawled, unconscious man. His body clamoured with pain; he put his mind against this and went staggering towards the cave's entrance, pausing just inside the mouth and having a long, intent look. He could see the ledge and the men milling upon it, and he could see the suspension bridge and the fringe of timber on the far side of the gorge. Despair rose in him; there was no escape this way, not when it would mean fighting his way through Conover's bunch to get to the bridge and across it.

The corral was on the far side of the gorge, he knew; Conover had left his horse there and carried his burden to the bridge, and after that others had come to help pack Larkin to the ledge. His gaze sweeping the far timber, Larkin caught the sheen of sunlight on moving horses and saw then where the corral was situated. The man who'd gone to fetch a rope had gone to that corral. Very shortly he'd be back.

Such was the situation, and it boded no good for Larkin. Yet this glimpse of ledge and bridge and corral had given him a full understanding of the nature of this hideout, and, because of that, he had his first faint hope. The cave had been fashioned by nature, and converted into a fortress by the bridge. The corral certainly wasn't handy, but it was better to have it situated on the far side of the canyon than to fight wild-eyed cayuses across that swaying terror of a bridge whenever a man came or went. In times of stress, of course, Conover could force the horses across the bridge and put them inside the cavern, if necessary; there was room enough in the cave and the horses would be out of danger if a posse, for instance, was laying siege along the far rim. The bridge could be cut by four knife strokes, Larkin judged, and in this easy manner Conover could make himself impregnable.

The flaw, of course, was that such a procedure would mean that Conover would be penned to the ledge and the cavern with no means of escape. And Larkin, certain that King Conover, too, would have long since considered this very factor, became just as certain that no such flaw existed. Conover had ridden this range when Dave Larkin had been one of Cultus Pierce's crew. Conover had had a reputation for wiliness even then. Therefore Conover was the kind of man to have provided himself against any exigency. And that meant that there must be an exit from the cavern.

Thus Larkin reasoned, and his eyes strayed to a small fire that burned on the ledge, and he saw that its smoke was drawn towards the cavern's mouth. Yet when Larkin turned and peered behind him, he saw nothing but blackness to the rear of the cave. The man on the floor groaned and stirred restlessly; Larkin looked again towards the ledge and the bridge, and he saw the second man shape up out of the timber on the far canyon rim, and the fellow came striding out upon the suspension bridge, a rope coiled over his arm.

Wheeling, Larkin faded silently back into the cave, facing towards its far end and finding that the walls pinched closer together as he progressed. Each step was taking him farther from the light that seeped in at the cave's mouth, and once he stumbled and almost fell; someone had left an old saddle lying back in here. He had a look behind him, and he saw the silhouette of a man in the entrance — the man with the rope. The walls were so close together now that Larkin could reach out and touch them on either side, the cavern had dwindled to a tunnel, and he might have reasoned that this tunnel was likely to come to a blank and abrupt end except that there was an air current to belie this supposition.

Then the tunnel angled abruptly, and he saw a dim eye of light ahead and above him.

He'd been climbing as he'd progressed deeper into the cave; he'd scarcely been conscious of this, but now the rocky floor tilted upwards at an angle that bent his back and put an ache in the calves of his legs. He sacrificed silence to effort, and he sent loose rocks rolling behind him, but he could see the sky ahead, and he came clawing out through the opening to find himself in a clump of bushes.

Up here on the barren crest of a hill, there were only a few stunted trees and no trail of any sort, and he knew why this exit had been left unguarded. There wasn't one chance in a thousand of anybody stumbling upon it from the outside. He forced his way out of the bushes and oriented himself; to the south, just over the brow of this hill, would be the sheer drop of the cliff to the ledge and canyon, so he stumbled off in another direction, staggering along with the certain knowledge that it would not be many minutes before the hue and cry would be raised.

From here he could look down upon a panorama of lesser hills and, beyond these, the sweep of the flats and the distant smoke of Swayback. Pine darkened these hills, and he moved downwards towards the timber. The railroad was a distant strand of sunlight across

115

the flatter land, losing itself in the hill country not far away. The canyon curved sinuously across his view, and the immensity of so much country made him feel small and tired and spent.

His disadvantage in the hunt that would come was that he did not know this particular section of the Silver Belts as Conover's men undoubtedly did; they'd anticipate him and move to hem him in, and the fact that no one had as yet appeared from the exit to give him chase only whetted his concern. Perhaps they'd crossed the canyon instead, to put some strategy of their own into operation. They'd give him no rest; he knew that. They'd need him alive for to-night's deal with Matt Hobbs, or, failing in that, they'd want him dead because of the knowledge of the cavern hideout he was now taking with him.

He got down the bald slope of the hill and into the timber and worked his way through it; his progress was slow and painful; the need for haste kept lashing him on, but he was light-headed at times and he stumbled often. He hadn't eaten for almost twenty-four hours, and thirst tormented him too, but at last he stumbled out of the timber to find himself at the canyon's lip. The gorge was shallower here than above, and the walls were less perpendicular. He moved along the rim until he found a game-trail that wended to the bottom. He had to be careful on that descent, but he made it, and he threw himself beside the creek at the gorge's bottom. He was prone upon the bank, sucking in his fill of water, when a rifle bullet geysered the water near him.

They were up on the far canyon wall above him — a dozen riders, and King Conover bulked big among them. They had searched him out, just as he'd feared, and he scrambled to a stand and ran for the willow that flanked the creek here at the gorge's bottom. He got himself screened, but still the bullets peppered about him. Then, suddenly, the rim above was empty. Hoofbeats hung on the still mountain air, a hawk wheeled silently overhead, all sound dwindling to nothing.

The water had revitalised him a great deal, but he was still hungry and he still ached from the beating he'd taken in Swayback, and he found trouble collecting his thoughts and pinning them to the needs of the situation. He knew that he must figure as King Conover was figuring; he knew he had to outmanoeuvre the pursuit, but clarity had forsaken him. He moved aimlessly down the canyon, keeping to the cover of the willows; gorge and creek broadened, and it came to him quite suddenly that he knew this water very well; it snaked across Cultus Pierce's acres to the east, and he had drunk from it many times in his cowboy days.

At last the canyon grew so wide that it ceased to be; he found himself in the timber of the lesser foothills. Behind him reared the mighty hill he'd descended, and he tried to gauge how far he'd come and was amazed at the miles. Then, afterwards, he discovered it was sundown; until now both time and distance had lost their meaning for him. He was thirsty again, and he tried to find the creek; he forsook such trails as existed and went clawing through the underbrush until he came upon a lightning-slashed tree that had an old and familiar look. He tried to recall where he'd seen such a tree before; it seemed very important to remember, and then he realised that he had passed it a scant half an hour before.

He was delirious now, and yet he still had moments when he was clear-headed enough to recognise his sickness and his danger. During one of these, he stood in silence and listened intently, and he heard a horse moving through the timber not far away. The sound faded as he strained his ears, but he heard a like sound, off in another direction. Those were Conover's men, he knew; they had fanned out and were combing the country for him. He began to laugh, softly. *Mustn't laugh*, he told himself. *Mustn't laugh or they'll hear you and come and ride you down.*

The sun was gone quickly behind the Silver Belts; the premature dusk of this hilly country brought a chill with it. He stumbled onwards through the darkness; the world had become a vastness of trees and shadows, and sometimes he heard men calling one to another. *That's them*, he told himself. *That's Conover's bunch, and they'll cling to the trail till they tack your hide on the wall.* He discovered that he'd said it aloud, and he laughed at that. He'd been alone too long, he decided. Only sheepherders talked to themselves!

The moon came rising, and the woods rustled to the stirring of its night life, and the wind sang in the pine tops, that soft, soothing refrain that was like a rush of lofty waters. He was hopelessly lost and too delirious to care about it. Possessed of his faculties he would have oriented himself and headed for a definite objective. He'd found a game-trail and was lurching along it; sometimes he stumbled and fell and crawled a few yards before he came to a stand again. In his clearer moments he realised he should avoid the trails; his only advantage over mounted men was that he could take to the underbrush. But he'd ceased to care.

He heard the rider who came towards him long before the horse shaped up out of the night. Another of Conover's men, he decided, and anger rose in him. A man got fed up with this hare and hounds business; he'd empty that saddle with a bullet, then show his heels to all of them with a horse between his knees. Hell, this was a dog-eat-dog game, and Conover's men had to take the chances, too. One bullet — and an end to stumbling and crawling and stumbling all over again.

Horse and rider came into view; he measured the distance along the moon-dappled trail and stepped out from the brush boldly. *Got to give him a chance,* he thought — *got to give the long-riding son a try at his gun.* His hand fell to his hip, his fingers groped in vain, but even then the fullness of his tragedy was not apparent to him. He only knew that his gun was gone, and he remembered then that it was in his war-sack. But where had he left his war-sack? Funny how memory tricked a man. So thinking, he laughed again. . . .

Melody, riding out of Swayback, kept at first to a steady, mile-eating pace, her objective the hills looming darkly to the west. Strong in her mind was all that had passed between herself and Amy Abbott, and sometimes she looked along the back trail, for Amy should be heading this way too, riding towards the Boxed-C. But the night was thick and dark now, and when the moon finally lifted itself to the east, Melody was off the rutted wagon road that led to the Pierce spread and was cutting directly overland to the foothills.

Desperation had sent Melody upon this ride, and when she contemplated her mission with a clearer head, she almost turned back. To comb the Silver Belts for Conover's hideout would be a futile task, but she was remembering things she'd heard said by Sig Kinsella in Nick Diamond's office this afternoon, and there'd been words that hadn't seemed significant then but which could now be shaped into something of value.

There's been a reference to Big Baldy — "I got back to town as fast as I could, boss. Nearly broke my fool neck coming down the slant of Big Baldy." Kinsella had ridden to Conover's hideout and back this day; he'd hurried to Swayback to fetch word that Larkin was in Conover's hands. And Melody, remembering all this now, knew that her search could be narrowed to the hill called Big Baldy.

She knew that landmark. She knew more about the country to the west of Swayback than she knew about the part of the town that lay north of the railroad tracks. Riding had occupied much of her time; she'd had her mornings and part of her afternoons to herself, and that one free evening a week, and she'd found sanctuary from the smoke and dust and clamour of Santone Street in riding the livery stable horses. Her profession put her before the crowd; in her own moments she turned naturally to solitude. To-night she found a value in the knowledge she'd thus gleaned.

Her trail took her to the north of the Boxed-C ranch buildings; she saw their lights across the flats, friendly and warm and heartening, and she remembered Amy again and wondered if it might not be wise to turn aside and join whatever rescue party was made up at the Pierce spread. Yet the desire to go on alone was stronger; she wondered about this and searched herself for the reason, and it came to her quite suddenly that it was born from her vague animosity towards Amy. She had come to Amy for help; she had gotten the promise of that help, yet now she wanted more than anything to be the one to find King Conover's hideout. She had given Amy the key that might mean Dave Larkin's rescue; now she wanted to snatch that key away from her. She, Melody, would locate the outlaw stronghold on Big Baldy, and then she would turn back to lead the Boxed-C men to it. Such was her plan, and it drove her onwards.

Beyond that, she didn't think. She knew that she was not far from the Boxed-C line shack where Matt Hobbs, with Crad Conover in tow, was to keep his rendezvous with the he-wolf of the hills; she had stopped at that line shack, deserted at this season, many times. She veered towards it now; she wanted to warn Matt Hobbs of the treachery that had been planned, to tell him a bullet would be all he'd get in exchange for Crad Conover, but when she reached the shack there was nobody about. At first she couldn't understand that; she sat her saddle in the moon-bathed clearing before the shack, listening intently and fighting down a growing fear, and then she remembered how hard she'd ridden. Matt Hobbs had left Swayback shortly before she, but she'd beaten him here. Or so she presumed.

Behind the shack, the hills loomed blackly; timber grew on all sides of the wide clearing, and she thought she saw movement at the fringe of the forest, off to her extreme left. She wished now that she'd come armed; she spurred her horse to action again and went around the shack and into the timber. Someone called, another voice answered, and she realised that more than one group of riders was in the vicinity. And since they couldn't be riders from the Boxed-C — not yet — it followed that they were Conover's men, gathered, she supposed, for the meeting with Matt Hobbs.

Then she knew that something about her presence here had excited them to alarm; there were more calls, and the sound of horses threshing through the timber to the right and to the left. It was nearly midnight, she judged; and she'd have given much in these fearsome moments to have seen Matt Hobbs shape up out of the darkness. But there was nothing to do but plunge onwards; she had found a trail of sorts, and she followed it blindly. She had to keep the horse to a walk; low-sweeping branches threatened to tear her from the saddle as it was, and, riding thus, she rounded a bend to find a man blocking her way.

He stood there in the moonlight filtering down through the trees; there was little of menace in his attitude; he seemed to be swaying on his feet. She didn't scream; she had had her bout with fear and it had been the fear of the unknown, the fear of shadowy pursuit through a shadowy forest. Here was something tangible, a foe to be fought, and she raised her quirt and brought it down as she swerved past him, and it was as she struck that she recognised him as Dave Larkin.

The lash caught him across a shoulder, and he went down beneath that blow, driven to his knees; and she kicked free of the stirrups and came falling off her horse, and the mount went galloping onwards. She got back to Larkin, and he lay crumpled in the trail, and she paused, not knowing what to do. Her heart was pounding rapidly; she could hear it, and she could hear something else as well — the steady beat of hoofs along the trail. Someone was coming! She got her hands under Larkin's armpits; he was more solid than she'd thought from the look of him, and she laboured at dragging him into the brush.

He'd only been dazed by her blow; he came to partial consciousness as she moved him, and he mumbled something that had no meaning. She said, "*Shhh.* They're coming. Conover's men." That must have percolated to him, for he rolled over and began crawling. They wormed their way into bushes which were thick and thorny, and they lay here, pressed close to each other, while two riders clattered past them on the trail.

Larkin's arm tightened around her, and he began babbling something about a cave and a bridge; his voice wasn't loud, but it put the fear in her again, and she got her fingers across his mouth. Keeping him silent, she strained her ears to every sound of the night and the woods; she could still hear men calling one to another, and the beat of hoofs, but those sounds were growing more distant. The search was moving away from them.

After that she could only wait in agonised impatience, listening . . . listening. . . . Then, gradually, she began to breathe easier, and some of the tenseness went out of her. They were safe for a while, at least, but Larkin seemed to be intermittently conscious and unconscious, and she knew that she didn't dare move him.

Moonlight reached its silvery fingers into these depths to touch his face. There was blood on it; some low-hanging limb had scratched him, or some rock of the trail when he'd stumbled. She unknotted her 'kerchief and dabbed the blood away, then tied the 'kerchief about his forehead. He moved closer to her, finding his way into her arms, and he said, "Amy . . . Amy. . . ."

She knew then how delirious he was, and she wondered if she dared leave him here alone while she tried to reach others who could come for him. He might try crawling away; he might stumble into the hands of Conover's men. She listened again; it had been half an hour since the pursuit had passed beyond, pressing deeper into the woods. Assured by the silence, she began to sing to Larkin, keeping her voice low. And, cradling him in her arms and crooning, she sensed that his breathing had become more regular, and she knew he'd lapsed into untroubled sleep. Once he opened his eyes; there seemed to be no fever in them now; and he looked at her intently for a long moment and then moved closer to her and went to sleep again.

She took to studying his face; the wind had browned it, and it was lined beyond his years, yet it was her thought that he was still a boy, and she marvelled that such a legend had been fashioned from such clay as this. But that was the way of all of them — the Dave Larkins and the Banjo Sorensons, and even the wild and vicious ones who pounded the Fandango's tables with their fists and tried to bully her into singing their favourite songs. They played hard at being men; they gloried in the tales that were tied to their names, but a woman's songs softened them and made them young again.

And then her song died abruptly, for again she heard hoofbeats along the trail.

Her first thought was that one of Conover's men was returning, but her intent listening told her that yonder was queer procedure for a man who was making a hunt. Then she understood. The horse out there was cropping beside the trail, moving a few steps from clump to clump of grass. She freed herself from Larkin and came to a cautious stand; she had a better look and recognised the horse as her own.

A wild elation made her heedless then. She tugged at Larkin; he mumbled a drowsy question and came to one knee. Half dragging him, she got him to the trail. She said desperately, "You've got to get up into that saddle! Here, let me help you reach the stirrup."

She wasn't sure that he understood her; he stood leaning against the horse, his eyes open but blankly uncomprehending. Then she heard more hoofbeats; there were riders in the timber all around them. That was her bleakest moment. There was no time now to get to the cover of the brush again.

When Amy Abbott had parted from Melody in Swayback, she had hurried into the house of Sheldon Abbott and gone directly to her own room. Here she changed to riding garb, moving with great haste but finding her fingers wooden. Dressed for the trail at last, she had a look at herself in the mirror. Excitement had put a glow to her cheeks, and she tried hard to calm herself; there was a bit of play-acting she had to do before she left here, and her audience would be a discriminating one. Minutes had become precious to her, and she waited with impatience for her pulse to cease its pounding, and then she went to face Sheldon Abbott.

She found him in his wheel-chair in the big living-room. Lamplight shed softly upon the scattered furnishings; this room was the hallmark of his opulence and his respectability. Chairs and table had graced his father's house and had come overland in high-sided freight wagons; a bookcase held volumes that were the accumulation of three generations, books whose very titles were without meaning to most of Swayback's citizenry. He was reading to-night some ponderous tome, and as she stood in the doorway regarding him it struck her that his must be a timeless world. Always he was like this, carefully shaved and properly groomed, a museum piece instead of a man, a living figure in a changeless tableau. And yet she wasn't sure. There was a vigour to him that made her feel that he might step from the wheel-chair if he so willed it; he was not born for inactivity, and he had always shaped his own destiny.

Seeing her, he dropped the book to his lap, marking his place with one long lean finger, and he said, "Good evening, my dear. You're going out to-night? Moonlight riding is a dull pastime when one rides alone. Or did I hear you talking with someone outside not long ago?"

That omniscience of his again! Or had he seen — and heard? She felt the colour come into her cheeks, and she was afraid to lift her eyes to the big window fronting the house from this room, afraid to try and see how great his visibility might have been from that window. She said casually, "Oh, yes. I was talking to one of dad's men. He rode in to say that dad wanted to see me to-night."

He frowned. "But we're going out to the Boxed-C for Sunday dinner."

"Whatever dad wants me about apparently can't wait," she said. "At least not as far as he's concerned. You know how he is. It will probably be some trifle that could have kept just as well. But we must humour him."

"Yes," he said. "We must humour him."

She crossed over to his chair and bent and kissed his cheek. Then she turned and hurried from the room and the house. At the barn behind the building, she saddled her own horse; it was a mount she had brought with her from the Boxed-C when she'd moved into town, and it had known more active days. It whinnied eagerly as she swung to the saddle, and she lifted it to a hard run once she'd put Swayback behind her. The thick darkness was fraught with no dangers for her; she knew this trail and had travelled it often.

She had the thought of Dave Larkin for company, and she wondered, with panic in her throat, if he were already dead. She had thought of Dave Larkin many times and in many ways, but she had never considered how it would be if the life were snuffed out of him. Now all of her relationship with him kept passing in review; she had known him as a lover in younger days; she had seen him leave to become a legend, and she had wondered about that, finding it hard to picture him as a town-tamer of the stature of Earp and Masterson.

True, she had considered him as dead once

before, at that time when Sheldon Abbott had told her of Larkin's passing in Dodge City, but that hadn't been like to-night. He'd been hazy and unreal then, grown dim in her memory, but his return to Swayback had made all that different. Yesterday she had speculated on what it had been like for him when he'd learned that she was Mrs. Sheldon Abbott. To-day she'd wondered where his trail would take him when he left here. That she would ride with him, in his heart, she was sure; he had told her as much in the Amarillo House without putting it into words. She had cherished that knowledge all of the day, and she had been honest enough with herself to admit that vanity kept the thought warm and glowing.

Now he was in danger, deadly danger, and she saw him anew and with adult eyes, and all of their relationship stood in stark nakedness, stripped of the garments of circumstance and convention. And, seeing him thus, she knew that she didn't want him to die. She remembered then what Melody had said, the girl's claim that any one once in love with Dave Larkin would always be in love with him. Here was the first hobble Amy had ever felt; she'd been the self-willed daughter of a father who was adamant in all things except those pertaining to her, and she wasn't sure that it was to her liking to be less her own mistress than she'd been. But the girl from the Fandango was no oracle, of course. The girl was in love with Larkin herself, and she tinged her observations with her own viewpoint and personality.

Thus Amy Abbott came to the facing of certain truths and refused to face them. And in this torment of reflection she rode across the prairie's flatness, rode with the moon rising behind her and the lights of her father's house gleaming to the west, and when she swung down from her horse before the gate leading into the ranch-yard, the animal was mottled with lather, and the rigours of that long, hard ride made Amy lurch as she came up a flagstone walk to the broad gallery fronting the house.

Cultus Pierce was in his living-room when she let herself inside. Here were bearskin rugs and cane-bottomed chairs, a crude table and a great-throated fireplace, black and cavernous, and the bigness of her father fitted into this raw and disorderly setting. He was hunched over the table, doing his accounts; figures had always remained a mystery to him, and his leathery old face was knotted into a frown, and the pencil in his hand was gnawed to a splintery shapelessness. He came to a quick stand when he saw her; something in the wild look of her must have helped him divine the urgency of her mission, for he said, "Amy! What is it?"

Her story came in disordered incoherence; there was jumbled mention of Matt Hobbs and Crad Conover and Dave Larkin and the he-wolf of the hills, but when it had tumbled out, he sensed the gist of the situation, and the need, and started past her for the door. But he paused for one question. He said, "Does your man know what fetched you out here to-night?"

She said, "Sheldon hates Dave. You know that. I told him you wanted to see me."

He said, "Tell him I needed a hand with those confounded ledgers." Then he was gone from the room and she stood leaning against the table, wishing she could cease her trembling. Outside, the ranch woke to an anarchy of sound. There was in her too great a restlessness to stand idly here, and she came out to the gallery and around it to where she could see men spilling from the bunkhouse and heading for the corrals. There was no sense, no direction to all this activity as far as the eye could see, yet out of it there came an orderly massing of men on horseback. When Cultus Pierce came riding up to the gateway, he was leading a saddled horse.

"Your cayuse can stand a rest, girl," he said.

I've turned it into the corral. Here's another for you. There'll be no talking you out of coming along, I reckon."

She didn't acknowledge his veiled hint that she stay behind; she came up into the empty saddle and they lined out, Pierce riding to the front with Amy at his side, and the dozen hands of the Boxed-C strung out behind them. They made a grim and silent cavalcade, and they veered steadily to the north-west as though their goal was fixed, but Amy had come alive to the futility of all this and she knew that her father had recognised from the first that it was a wild goose chase to comb the high hills for a man of King Conover's ilk. Yet there was one bit of solidness to fasten on to; the Boxed-C's north line shack had been the place of rendezvous, and it was there her father was heading, Amy now realised.

They found the line shack as Melody had found it, the clearing around it moon-bathed, the structure standing stark against the backdrop of the pine-shadowed hills, the place deserted. There was a heavy silence here; the pines sang to the wind's soft strumming, that and nothing more. Pierce cupped his big hands to his mouth and called tentatively, "Hobbs? Matt Hobbs?"

Off at a distance there was a faint stirring, and two men shaped up out of the underbrush afoot. One limped and led the other by a short bit of rope placed around the prisoner's neck. Crad Conover was still handcuffed, and now he was gagged with a bandanna as well. Amy recognised Hobbs' shapeless slicker before she recognised the man. Hobbs said cautiously, "Boxed-C — ?"

Cultus Pierce expelled a gusty sigh of relief. When Hobbs had come into the circle of horsemen, Pierce looked at him in the bright moonlight and said, "Better get that buzzard's son back to your calaboose, Matt. There'll be no swap to-night. The only thing King Conover has got for you is a bullet."

Hobbs smiled. "I'd judged as much. Ye savvy how it is with an old man, Cultus? When I was young and my hide was worth hanging on to, I treated it like I could buy another for a plugged peso. Now I'm a mite more careful. I left the horses hobbled back a piece and then hid out in the brush. King Conover and his men showed up around here not long ago, but Dave Larkin weren't with 'em."

Amy quickened with interest. "You think Dave got away from them?" she asked. "Or were they bluffing about having him in the first place?"

"No bluff, Amy," Hobbs said. "Not long ago somebody rode up to this shack, but I couldn't tell who. Either a girl or a kid, I'd reckon, from the build. Conover's men gave chase; they all headed into the timber over there."

The wave of his arm obliterated the shack and indicated the trees behind it. "Ye'll find fair hunting in those woods, I'm thinking."

Pierce said, "You hear him, boys? We'll be riding." He glanced down at Hobbs. "Take young Conover to my place, Matt," he said. "I'll send a couple of my boys back into Swayback with you later to-night — just to play safe."

Hobbs said, "One minute, Cultus. How did ye know ye'd find me here with Crad Conover?"

Pierce grinned without a great deal of humour. "Matt, I ain't asking you who gave you authority to take a prisoner out of the calaboose with the idea of turning him loose to-night."

They were alike, these two; they had been schooled by Texas and by the trail north, and they understood each other; Amy could see that. Hobbs said, "Good hunting, Cultus. I'll hold down your ranch until ye get back."

Pierce lifted his leonine head like an animal come alert to the nearness of prey, and then he spurred his horse forward; behind him his men fanned out, and in this manner they spread a living net as the timber swallowed them. They needed no orders, these Boxed-C riders; they had hunted King Conover's crew before. They couldn't hope for silence; the woods livened to the crashing of men and mounts along the timbered trails. Amy stayed close behind her father, who picked his careful way, bending low in his saddle and warning her whenever a limb barred the way. He grunted once and said, "Ain't a Chinaman's chance of finding anything back in here. They've moved away from us, sure as shooting."

That brief meeting with Matt Hobbs had lifted her spirits; the cold logic of Cultus Pierce dropped them again. Then they came around a turn to see, dimly, the man and woman and horse standing before them. The man sagged against the horse, the woman was trying to help him into the saddle. Amy cried, *"Dave!"* She came down out of her saddle and ran forward, and Pierce made a ponderous descent and was close behind her. It was he who caught Larkin in his arms, and he said, "Look to the girl, Amy! I think she's going to faint."

Melody said weakly, "I'm all right. It was just the shock. I thought you were Conover's men come back for him."

Pierce said, "Dave's out like a light." He raised his voice in a reaching bellow. *"Boxed-C! Over thisaway. I've found him!"*

And so they came to this meeting in the darkness of the woods; men gathered to surround the little knot of rescued and rescuers until they were in each other's way, and their babbled questions made bedlam. Pierce said, "Here, some of you give me a hand. We'll carry him back to the line shack and see if we can get him in shape to sit a saddle."

They moved out of the woods with their horses led behind them and Larkin supported by many arms, and in the full moonlight that lay beyond this fringe of timber, Melody climbed to the saddle of her horse. Cultus Pierce had his first real look at her now, and he said, "I don't reckon I'd know you."

Amy said, "She's the one who told me about Dave and King Conover, Dad."

"I make my living at the Fandango," Melody said. "I'm going back there now. There is a great deal you probably want to know. I'm sorry that I can't tell you more than I have." She glanced at the unconscious form of Larkin. "He means something to you folks, I know. If you're obligated to me for helping him, you can forget about my part in what happened to-night. Do I make myself clear?"

Pierce said, "I'm thinking that what you learned, you learned in the Fandango. You don't want Nick Diamond to know that you bought in. He won't, girl. I speak for myself and my men."

Melody's glance fastened upon Amy; there was no reading Melody at this moment. She said, "He's been badly used to-day, Mrs. Abbott. He'll need care. Lots of care."

Then she'd wheeled her horse and was gone galloping across the moonlit plain; they watched her as long as they could, Amy's eyes fathomless, her father's dark with bewilderment. Amy broke the spell by saying, "We'd better get Dave home."

They hoisted Larkin into a saddle made empty by two men doubling up on another horse; they supported him on either side and took a longer, slower trail on their return trip to the Boxed-C. The ranch-house glowed brightly when they came to it; Matt Hobbs greeted them at the door, took his look and said, "Larkin, eh! And alive. A good night's work, Cultus."

"We'll get him into my bed and see how much damage has been done him," Pierce said. "Lend a hand, Matt. What did you do with young Conover? How's that? Handcuffed out in the bunk-house, eh? Amy, go to the cook-shack and have that slant-eyed heathen make up some broth in a hurry. Tell him that if it isn't ready to spoon into Dave in fifteen minutes, I'll have his yellow skin off him and his bones strewing unhallowed ground. Now step, girl!"

He was in his element now, was old Cultus; there was work for his hands. With Hobbs helping him, they got Larkin undressed and into bed, and they went over his naked body inch for inch, probing and scrutinising. Hobbs said then with a sigh, "No bullet wounds and no broken bones, I'd judge. But he's black and blue and scratched up like he'd tangled with a bob-wire fence. And that mark on his shoulder couldn't have come from anything but a quirt. But rest and care will bring him around."

Larkin opened his eyes then. In them was a brief bewilderment at finding himself in strange surroundings, but it was followed by a weary contentment. He said, "Howdy, Cultus, you old son-of-a-gun."

Pierce said, "You'll take a lot of killing, Davy boy," and was delighted beyond measure.

Amy came in with a steaming bowl of broth. She smiled and said, "Hallo, Dave. Awake, I see. Here, just wait till I feed this to you."

She seated herself by the bed, and he was able to free his arms from under the blanket, but she could see that any movement was hard for him. The broth brought the life back into him, though, and he said, "Just what all happened? I remember miles and miles of walking, and then somebody hiding me out in the brush. Some things are clear, some are foggy. . . ." His eyes strayed to Matt Hobbs, who stood on the opposite side of the bed. "Matt!" he said. "You swapped Crad Conover —"

Hobbs shook his head. "I fetched him to make the trade, Dave, but it weren't necessary. He goes back to Swayback's calaboose to-night. King Conover spun himself a mighty good scheme, but it didn't work. Ye'll be well enough to ride away in a few more days."

Larkin closed his eyes, and that let the rush of memory come. It was all turning clear again — the fight at the water tank in Swayback, that painful ride on a box-car's hard planking, his getting off the train at another water tank, high in the Silver Belts, his escape from Conover's cavern hideout.

He saw all these things once more, but he saw more than that. There was the chain of circumstances that had brought him in a wide circle from Swayback to the hills and almost back again. There was the loyalty of a man who'd been willing to tarnish his badge by trading the law's prisoner for a town-tamer who'd come to Swayback only to ride out again. There was the courage of another man and his daughter who had ridden this night for him. And thinking of how it had been with all of them, he knew now that there was indeed a touch of the cavalier in him; he knew that a man couldn't turn his back upon the kind of debt he'd incurred here. Not with honour.

And so he said, "There's two things I'll be wanting, Matt. A chance to sleep the clock around in this bed. And your badge. If you're through with it, Matt, I'd like to take a whack at being marshal of Swayback. I owe you something."

Hobbs had that old hope in his eyes again, but he had his kind of honour too. He said, "It was me that was paying off when I fetched Crad Conover out of Swayback. Ye owe me nothing, Dave."

"No?" Larkin said. "Then put it this way: I've got an account to square with Santone Street. But you don't understand about that. Give me the badge, Matt. I'll keep it until I've a shirt to pin it on to."

"So Larkin is taking the marshal's badge," Sheldon Abbott said.

They were alone in the big living-room of the frame house, he and Amy; afternoon's sunlight spread a misshapen diamond upon the carpet, but Abbott kept the wheel-chair in the shadows. Amy sat rigidly in a high and straight-backed chair; the marks of a sleepless night put a smudge beneath her eyes and made her face older. She said, "I've told you all I know, Sheldon. The doctor thinks that Dave should stay out at dad's place at least a week, and of course dad won't hear of Dave's being moved. Yes, he's taking the badge. Isn't that what you wanted?"

Smiling, Abbott lifted his eyes from his blanket-wrapped lap; he had a penetrating way of looking at her, and she flinched beneath it. "Of course, my dear," he said. "And he'll do Swayback a great deal of good, I'm sure. You must arrange to have him here for dinner when he's up and about. We'll not be going out to the Boxed-C on Sunday, as originally planned. Your father will understand that we wouldn't want to disturb the patient."

She had grown steadily more uncomfortable with the feeling that she was being toyed with; she had known this feline cruelty of Sheldon Abbott's before, but she was so tired that it took an effort to be defiant. But she said, "Something has been bothering you ever since I came home this morning, Sheldon. Now you're playing with words, and you've been too polite. For heaven's sake, say it!"

This was not according to the rules; their eternal sparring had always followed a faithful ritual in which bluntness was akin to blasphemy, and he turned silent before the challenge in her voice. Contrition softening her, she crossed to the low stool beside his chair and seated herself and leaned gently against his knees. She said in a kinder voice, "What is it, Sheldon?"

There was no reading his long, wedge-like face. But: "Am I presumptuous, my dear," he said, "in considering it an odd coincidence that your business at the Boxed-C last night brought you there at the very hour when your father took his crew towards the Silver Belts in search of Larkin? There are too many missing pages, Amy. For instance, just what gave Cultus Pierce the idea that Larkin was in Conover's hands and in danger?"

She'd had much time to prepare the story she'd told him in detail this afternoon, and she'd thought it had sounded plausible enough. The very loopholes that had been left were to have given it the ring of truth; if it had been too tightly woven he would have been quick to suspect that it had been partly manufactured. Or so she had reasoned. That omniscience of his had awed her before; now she found herself frightened.

She said hastily, "I've told you that dad sent for me because he needed help with his accounts. Whatever he learned about Dave Larkin being in trouble, he must have learned in the meantime. All I know is that he was ready to ride when I arrived, and I rode with him. I've explained about Matt Hobbs and Crad Conover, and the swap Hobbs was going to make. Maybe Hobbs stopped at the Boxed-C first and told dad what was up. You'll have to ask dad for the details."

"Which I won't do, of course," he said. "One doesn't pry into the affairs of Cultus Pierce. And Matt Hobbs won't talk either — not if he doesn't wish to. It would seem that Hobbs' last official act as marshal was unofficial, but I suppose there's no harm done since Crad Conover is back in his cell."

Still smiling, he looked down at her. "Forgive me, my dear, for an invalid's suspicions. You've told me all you know about last night, I'm sure. But" — his fingers closed on her arm, and she was astonished at his strength — "please remember this, Amy. I shall need you to help handle him, to make sure that he conducts his office in the manner of our choosing. Perhaps we'll be seeing a great deal of him. Remember that I'll be watching, my dear . . . watching. . . ."

She said, "You're hurting my arm!" He released his grip and lifted his hand to her hair and began stroking it with the old, gentle gesture that was still somehow possessive. But the mark of his fingers still marred the fairness of her skin, and, looking at the dull red blotches, she saw Sheldon Abbott as she'd never seen him before. There was violence in him, more violence than she'd suspected, and strength, too. She'd thought of him only as a brain and a personality; she knew now that he was elemental beneath that fine veneer. And the knowledge was awesome and terrifying and wonderful.

The Chinaman's sat midway of Swayback's main street, a long, low, narrow building with a counter and stools, and a few tables at the far end of the single room. The aroma of frying foods clung constantly to the place; flies droned beyond the screen doors, and the clatter of dishes made a ceaseless symphony, rising and falling as the day dragged onwards.

147

In this mid-afternoon hour, Judge Joshua X. Bragg, sitting in solitary dignity at one of the tables and spending an inordinate amount of the town's time at dawdling over a cup of coffee, spied Matthew Hobbs in the front doorway and beckoned to him. Hobbs paused for a few words with the Chinaman and then limped to Bragg's table and seated himself. The day was warm, but Hobbs was still wearing his long yellow slicker. Bragg said, "So your long service has finally been terminated, suh. Dave Larkin is marshal of Swayback."

Hobbs looked tired. "I'm a sort of deputy now, ye see — handling things for him here until he's on his feet. 'Tis a tray I'm after for Crad Conover. We'll want him fat and sassy when we give him a trial and hang him."

Bragg nodded speculatively. "A good night's work, suh. I've been mulling over the things you told me after your return from the Boxed-C this morning. Larkin's account, suh, of Conover's hideout and his escape from it are very interesting."

"Dave was unconscious on the way to the cave, and mighty delirious after he escaped," Hobbs observed. "Just the same, I'm thinking we can cut sign on that outlaw nest from what Dave told me. At least the search would be considerably narrowed down."

Bragg produced a piece of paper. "I, suh,

148

have prepared a map based upon the information you gleaned. A map is the military approach to any objective. Did I tell you, suh, that I served under the late General George A. Custer? If I hadn't been incapacitated by a bullet wound received in a previous campaign, I would have ridden with the Seventh to its rendezvous with death at the Little Big Horn and —"

"Ye told me," Hobbs interjected wearily and mopped his brow. "I'm thinking, Judge, that Conover's hideout is of no real concern to us. Cultus Pierce heard Dave talk, and Cultus will smoke out the old he-wolf sooner or later. Larkin told me that his first move as marshal will be to close the Fandango, run Nick Diamond and his crew out of town, and padlock any other place on Santone Street that proves to need padlocking. Ye'll do well to worry about the trouble Swayback will be seeing before the smoke clears away."

"A judicious outlook," Bragg conceded. "But what of the friends Conover has here? Remember the scholarly hand of the note that purported to come from King Conover yesterday? And now, suh, we know that Larkin was not snatched from Swayback by Conover, but was beaten and placed in a box-car by Sig Kinsella and others from the Fandango. Have you thought, suh, that it might have been Nick Diamond's fine hand we read in that note? My point, suh, is that Santone Street and the high hills may have an alliance that makes Conover as worthy of our consideration as the Fandango. Possibly the same thought has crossed Larkin's mind."

"If it has, Dave's keeping the notion to himself," Hobbs said. "All I can do is wait until Larkin's in town. He's the big boss from here on out. Ye'll notice that the Chinaman has my tray ready. 'Tis a late meal for Crad Conover, but it will do him good to wait. Good day, Judge."

Crad Conover, lounging against the barred door of his cell, glanced with an impatient man's quick anger as Matt Hobbs came limping along the jail's corridor with the tray.

"Now that Dave Larkin's taken your badge," Conover said, "I was beginning to wonder if I was gonna have to wait until he was on his feet and in town before I got fed."

Hobbs slid the tray through the aperture designed for that purpose. "It's late, but it's better food than the crow your brother is eating to-day," he said.

Turning away after making his thrust, Hobbs went limping up the corridor and out of the building, and Crad Conover watched him go, his eyes thoughtful and the anger rising in him. He knew what Hobbs had meant, did Crad Conover. He had been taken from this jail the night before, and he hadn't understood then why Hobbs had led him to the hills. But he'd pieced out part of the truth while he'd waited gagged and bound as Hobbs kept a lonely vigil near the line shack, and he'd learned the whole of the matter when he'd listened to the talk between Hobbs and Cultus Pierce a little later.

Yes, there'd been a good scheme, but it hadn't worked. Dave Larkin, in King Conover's hands, had been a hostage who was to have been exchanged for the King's brother — but something had gone wrong. King Conover had meant to swap Larkin for Crad, then put a bullet into the town-tamer and another into Hobbs, but the truth had seeped out, and the wariness of Matt Hobbs and the arrival of Cultus Pierce had spoiled the play. A few hours before, Crad Conover had been shackled in the Boxed-C bunk-house, impotent prey to the taunts of Pierce's crew. Now he was back in Swayback's jail.

King Conover had failed him, and a broken-down old mossyhorn like Matthew Hobbs could laugh at the Conovers, for Dave Larkin was safe, and Larkin had accepted the marshal's badge. Crad had learned that, too, before he'd left the Boxed-C. The audacity of King Conover had come to naught; worse than that, it would make the law of Swayback warier. No longer would King Conover's men dare to ride into town to talk to the King's brother through the cell window. In less than twenty-four hours, Crad's chances of being freed had diminished immeasurably.

He hadn't eaten since this morning at the Boxed-C; he'd waited ravenously for the food Matt Hobbs had been so long in bringing, but now, with the steaming tray on the floor, Crad Conover turned away from it and crossed his cell and put his browned hands on the window bars and tested them gingerly. But even such wiry strength as his couldn't budge them.

He fell to pacing; he knew now that he must plan to escape; no longer could he be content to merely sit here, waiting for the King's coming. His trial was scheduled for less than two weeks away, and a town emboldened by Dave Larkin's acceptance of the law's badge would give him swift justice. His fingers strayed to his throat; for a moment an overpowering panic surged through him and he wanted to throw himself against the barred door and hammer at it with all his strength. He thought, *"Steady! Steady!"* and was surprised to find that he'd whispered aloud.

There had to be a way. There could be a way. They hadn't built the jail yet that could hold a Conover. Egotism flowered to conquer his fear; the pride of his wildling strain squared his shoulders and took the trembling out of his hands. He'd be watching from here on out. He'd be waiting. . . .

"And now we've got Dave Larkin wearing Matt Hobbs' badge," Nick Diamond said with a vast disgust and kicked a pebble over the rim of the gorge. The rock, striking the perpendicular wall, made a sharp sound and then went falling towards that thread of a creek far below and was lost to sight.

Hard riding had brought Diamond here to the canyon hideout of King Conover; his horse and Sig Kinsella's, in the hidden corral across the gorge, were lathered by the long trail from Swayback to the high hills, and both weariness and worry had sagged Diamond's slight frame and greyed his handsome face. He stood at the ledge end of the suspension bridge, Kinsella lounging close by while King Conover and his men squatted beside the small fire. None of them spoke, and Diamond, a trace of petulance in his voice, said, "Can't you understand what I'm telling you? Larkin's town marshal now!"

King Conover lifted his craggy face, and his eyes met and held Diamond's. "You're here to kick, feller, and you've got a right to," Conover said. "My luck clabbered on me yesterday. I got careless with Larkin, and he got away. I'll not make that same mistake again. Hobbs fooled me, too; he was smart enough to keep himself hid until I was ready to show my hand. And with Larkin gone I had no card to play. But there was a leak some place, Nick. I've told you the whole story. Who was it rode up to the Boxed-C line shack and got chased by my boys? It was either a kid or a girl, from the build."

"A kid or a girl . . . ?" Diamond mused, then suddenly stiffened with suspicion.

Kinsella regarded his boss with quick appraisal. "Why don't you say it, Nick?" he challenged. "She took last night off to go riding. You told me so yourself. Said she didn't feel up to giving a good performance. Maybe now I'm understanding how Dave Larkin come to have a deck of cards from the Fandango when he showed up in Bragg's court."

Diamond said softly, "Perhaps you're right, Sig. Perhaps you're right. We'll find out about that. We'll give her enough rope to hang herself. I'm more concerned with Dave Larkin right now."

Kinsella glanced at Conover and said, "If you'd only let me put a bullet into him, King, like I wanted —"

Conover came to a stand, big and rocky and dwarfing both Kinsella and Diamond. A

154

blasted hope and a night's futile riding had shortened his temper, and he said, "I ain't of a mind to listen to what I should have done and didn't. If you're here to talk of what's ahead, that's different. Otherwise you're just burning daylight."

Diamond smiled his soft and bewitching smile. "You're right, King. Spilt milk is spilt. And you've as much to worry about as any of us. Larkin's seen this hideout. Are you staying here long?"

"Till I'm run out. Finding us here will be one thing. Smoking us out will be another. You'll notice that the Boxed-C hasn't killed any horses getting up here to-day. You're the one, Nick, who's got to decide whether to stay or move. We don't know how much Larkin heard here on the ledge. Maybe he's wise to that bank job we've got in mind — maybe he isn't. But any way you look at it, Santone Street's a hotter spot than this ledge right now."

Diamond said, "He's going to try driving me out. Already the town is telling it that his first move will be against the Fandango. And they're quoting what Larkin told Hobbs when they say it. What's more, the town will back Larkin — something they didn't do for Matt Hobbs. There's been war-talk ever since Larkin heaved me through Judge Bragg's window. That's what comes of having a reputation like Larkin's; rabbit-hearted men borrow courage on the strength of it. The next move is Larkin's."

"I know his breed," Conover said. "He'll do business according to the badge-toter's way. He'll come and give you your chance to get out. He'll set a day and an hour, and after that he'll come with smoke. And what will you do when he names your deadline?"

"Running makes a bad habit," Diamond said. "Horseback news travels fast and wide. If I leave Swayback, I'll leave every town I hit."

Conover said, "Once he calls for a showdown with you, get the word to me. We'll play his own scheme against him, Nick. When the hour comes, he'll head south of the tracks, and those that call themselves fighting men will be at his back. Do you see it now? That's the very hour I'll strike at the bank and bust Crad out of jail. They'll have two chunks of trouble on their hands at once. And when Abercrombie's vault is empty and Crad is in a saddle, we'll be turning south to lend you a hand. They won't be expecting that. And it will be our town when the smoke settles."

Diamond gave this due consideration, taking his time at it, for he knew a showdown when he saw one shaping, and everything was at stake now. At last he smiled. "It's pat, King," he said. "It's pat. Come on, Sig. Let's be riding."

Cultus Pierce, thrusting his leonine head through the doorway of the bedroom in his Boxed-C ranch-house and finding Larkin awake, said, "How's the new town marshal this afternoon?"

Larkin, propped up against pillows, smiled. "Fine, Cultus. I could use a man-size beefsteak. That Chinaman of yours has spooned enough broth into me to float a Missouri River side-wheeler. If you're sure the doctor has hit the trail to Swayback, I'll slip into my pants."

Frowning, Pierce said, "You'll stay in that bed if I have to hog-tie you. At least a week. Man, do you think you're made of iron? Swayback can wait a while for your brand of lawing."

His mood changing, he advanced into the room and seated himself upon the edge of the bed. There was a hominess here, made of hooked rugs and framed tintypes and a wallpaper that had had the garishness taken out of it by time. The springs creaking beneath his weight, Pierce said, "It's good to have you here again, son."

Larkin sighed. He had thought himself immune to nostalgia; he had thought that the disappointment of a changed Swayback had put him beyond homesickness, but there were things without change, and the personality of Cultus Pierce was one of these. He said, "It's good to be back, Cultus. Even if only for a little while."

Pierce turned silent; one horny finger traced the pattern of the quilt, and Larkin, recognising that the man had something to say and was hard put for the proper words, said, "What is it, Cultus?"

Pierce said, "Amy, Dave. Is she the reason you asked for Matt Hobbs' badge?"

"Don't know," Larkin said slowly. "I don't think so. Once she asked me to stay, and I refused her. Yet she knew me better than I know myself. She told me that I wouldn't turn away from Swayback's need, and I didn't. Yet Matt Hobbs is mixed up in it too. And you. And Nick Diamond."

Pierce said incongruously, "You didn't know Amy's mother, Dave. She died when Amy was small. She was a good woman, son, but she was cursed with ambition. She got that from her folks; they could have bought and sold the Pierces with their fooforaw money. Why she ever picked me to marry, I'll never know, and I'll always be humble, just thinking about it. And she made me, Dave. Long before I realised the truth, she saw that

Texas grass was growing thin from overgrazing and that there'd be poor pickings in the days to come. She got me to look for virgin graze in Montana, and she talked me into experimenting with better breeds than the longhorn. This Boxed-C is made of my sweat, but it's the stuff of her dreaming, just the same."

He was an old man, talking more to himself than to his listener; or so Larkin sensed. His eyes were misty with looking backwards across long years, yet there was more here than meditation and remembrance, and this Larkin sensed also. So he said, "What are you trying to tell me, old-timer?"

"You and me parted once with hot words, son," Pierce said. "I drove you off this ranch because Amy was too interested in you. You hated me for that; you told me so. You figgered I thought you weren't good enough to lick her boots. There was more to it than that, Dave. Whenever I look at her, I see her mother. Now she's married to Sheldon Abbott; maybe she likes that, maybe she doesn't; she married him more out of pity than anything else after his accident. But he's her kind of man, just the same. She'll live to learn that. Look at him now — mayor of Swayback at his age. Another ten years and he'll likely be Montana's governor. Then it will be the

United States Senate. Either that, or he'll stay here and build Swayback up to his size. Either way, he's got the right wife for the job."

Dave thought he understood then, and his pity was for Pierce. He said, "And now I've come back. . . ."

"Another five years and that wouldn't have made any difference," Pierce said. "Amy will know her mind then; she's her mother's daughter, and blood will have told. I've seen that coming since she was old enough to walk. Your kind of ambition and hers wouldn't be the same."

Larkin said, "She's married to another man. I won't be forgetting that. Neither will Amy. Chalk this down, Cultus; you'll never have to worry about my spoiling her life."

Pierce looked at him, his leathery old face crinkled with surprise. "Dave, boy," he said, "you don't savvy what I've been trying to say. It's *you* I've been worried about."

And so, through that long day, the news that Dave Larkin had elected to stay and had taken the badge of Marshal Matthew Hobbs spread as wildfire spreads, fanned by a prairie breeze. It had swept through Swayback, a tale enlarged by many tellings; it had gone along the street where respectability reigned; it had seeped south to Santone Street. It had entered

160

the high frame house of Sheldon Abbott, and it had been carried to the craggy Silver Belts. Many men had heard it, and each had reacted in his own way, measuring this thing as it would pertain to himself. Fear had given wing to the news — fear and worry and hope and doubt. Emotions had caught fire from a wilder flame, some to flare fitfully, some to rise to a roaring height. . . .

There was the one man, though, who found this beyond his interest, the man whose own flame burned to the exclusion of all else, for to Banjo Sorenson, Dave Larkin was merely a man who had helped him out of a tight spot and then walked out of his life. Loyalty had been born at their meeting, and gratitude too, but there was room for only one driving interest in Sorenson, and that interest had consumed him.

Yes, he had heard, but the news had carried little meaning to him. Now, in the heat of mid-afternoon, he sat upon the edge of a boardwalk in upper Santone Street, a small boy hunkered beside him, and Sorenson was hard at the task of talking. He'd learned patience, had Sorenson, and a measure of wiliness. These things now fashioned his speech for him.

"You ban Yimmy Davis's best friend," he was explaining carefully. "All the little fellers say that if anybody knows where Yimmy got these spurs, it ban you. Maybe you afraid for to tell me, eh? Maybe you t'ink it gets trouble for you, eh?" He smiled a friendly, doggish smile. "See here? Two-bits. Now you tell me what I want to know."

The boy dug a bare toe into the dust of the street, tracing a weird and lopsided pattern. "Four-bits?" he said hopefully.

Sorenson made no show of his wild surge of exultation. "A bargain," he agreed.

"Jimmy and me stole 'em," the boy said. "We sneaked into the Fandango one day and into one of those upstairs rooms. This one was being used by some jigger to sleep in. We was hopin' we might find some loose change lying around. Those spurs was under the bed. Jimmy was to wear 'em one week and me the next. That was the deal."

Excitement swept away all of Sorenson's calculated show of only casual interest, and he bobbed to his feet, saying, "Vich room? Vich room? You take me there!"

He'd frightened the boy; he saw that instantly. The youngster scooted away at an angle and paused with this margin of safety between them. "I don't know which room. I was too scared to notice. All I wanted was to get out of there fast."

Sorenson said, "Don't be afraid."

"The four-bits, mister," the boy reminded him.

Sorenson sent the coin spinning through the air, and he still stood after the boy had scurried away, though he didn't notice the departure. His eyes were on the distant flamboyant front of the Fandango; he stared long and intently, his face wooden, his great hulk of a body motionless. Then he went to where he'd left his horse, and a half-hour later found him on the trail to the Boxed-C, a decision made.

Many men north of the tracks had to-day pledged their loyalty to Dave Larkin, making mighty promises to back him in whatever his play might be. One man rode now to offer himself as a deputy. For the Fandango was the recognised citadel of those who would oppose Dave Larkin's law, and the Fandango also housed the man who owned all of Banjo Sorenson's hate. Thus had the needs of the two joined. Thus had the die been cast.

Larkin, riding stiffly in the saddle, returned
to Swayback on a borrowed Boxed-C horse
a week from the day he had stumbled down
from the Silver Belts, hunted and delirious.
Long confinement to a bed had thinned him
down to gauntness and put hollows in his
cheeks and softened the tan of his face, but
the real change went deeper. Since last he'd
seen the false fronts of Swayback he'd accepted
a badge, and the solemn responsibility of that
acceptance had given him an inward stature
and an inward bleakness.

Also, he had acquired a deputy, and the
choice had gone against his better judgment.
To Banjo Sorenson's plea, made in the
Boxed-C ranch-house bedroom almost a week
before, he had listened with only ordinary interest. To Sorenson's tale of a tragic visit and
a girl left ravished and dead, he had turned
a more attentive ear. He knew then, did Larkin, when the yarn was spun, why the Scandinavian had been so agitated by sight of that
broken spur in Judge Bragg's court-room, and
he knew, too, why the light and laughter had
been burned out of Sorenson.

Here was a hatred that was both ice and

flame, yet there was this one small part of Sorenson it had not yet consumed. The man was law-abiding by nature, therefore he wanted the sanction of the law in his hour of vengeance. Hence the appeal for a deputy's badge. Judge Bragg had been mistaken when he'd schemed with Matt Hobbs to have Sorenson banished from town for fear the giant would blindly rush to his own doom. Banjo Sorenson was bent upon playing his last card carefully.

And so Larkin had promised him a badge, but not without misgivings. A deputy he could use, yes, but a man had to be impersonal about this business of town-taming; he had to treat it as a job, not as a crusade. You could be a cavalier, come riding out of the cactus, but whatever the instinct that prompted you, you had to be cold and soulless as a six-shooter when the work was being done. True, in Larkin's own case Nick Diamond's order that had sent him out of Swayback a beaten man had prompted Larkin to accept a challenge. But, trained in these things, he had already banished his personal animosity to a corner of his mind. With Sorenson it would be different. Yet Larkin had given his word.

Into Swayback, he came riding along that newer business street, past the mercantile stores and the blacksmith shop and livery and saloon and bank, and he lighted unobtrusively at the hitching-rack before the frame building that was Swayback's town hall, and then crossed over to the jail. He found Matt Hobbs in the little ante-room that fronted the building — Hobbs and Banjo Sorenson who sat stolidly upon a chair in one corner. The greetings over, Hobbs said, "He's come here every day, Dave, waiting for you to show up. Says he's a deputy now."

Larkin said, "See if you can scare him up a spare badge, Matt."

Hobbs said, "Your own is still unofficial. Sheldon Abbott has got to appoint ye, but that's just a formality. Abbott said to have you come over for supper the day ye hit town. He'll do the honours then."

Larkin nodded. "Get word to him that I'll be along this evening."

"Your guns are here on the desk," Hobbs went on. "I had your war-sack fetched from the Santone Street livery stable."

Larkin took guns and belt and holsters into his hands. Time and use had dulled the leather and the steel; the trigger-dogs of the forty-fives were filed to split-second smoothness. Testing the weapons, Larkin loaded five cylinders in each, spun them, latched the belt around his waist and settled the guns against his hips. He supposed that a moment like this called for some sort of ceremony, a significant gesture or an adequate speech. He was conscious of the solemn gaze of Hobbs and Sorenson, but all he said was, "I'm heading for Santone Street."

Hobbs' tufted eyebrows arched. "So soon?"

"I've wasted a week, Matt. Come along, Banjo."

They went shoulder to shoulder, walking to the tracks and across them and towards that double row of weathered, close-crowding buildings, and soon they were striding along Santone Street, moving at an even pace from the shadows of wooden awnings to the sunlit stretches between, bucking a slow-moving current of men, but drawing no attention to themselves, and it was not until they'd reached the batwings of the Fandango that Larkin broke the silence. He said then, "I'll do the talking, Banjo."

Here in this dust Jimmy Davis had died, and from yonder window of the Amarillo House Larkin had watched him die. He drew a measure of determination from that recollection, and he shouldered inside, blinking to adjust his eyes to the lesser light. Smoke lay in blue layers above a bar that flanked one wall from end to end of the building; here a mammoth mirror doubled the battalion of bottles lined before it. To the right-hand side of the vast room were gaming tables, and at the far end was a tiny stage, its faded curtain closed. The piano was down there by the stage, its music clanking steadily, monotonously; and a rumble of sound rose from the men at tables and bar.

Nick Diamond was here, his back to his own bar, his elbows propped against the mahogany, and Sig Kinsella was at his side. Towards them Larkin walked; he knew that Sorenson was at his heels, but the Swede had dropped back, beyond Larkin's range of vision. Diamond saw them first but made no move; Kinsella, slower of perception, came out of his slouching position and to a nervous alertness. Diamond's smile stayed soft and bewitching. He said, "Hallo, Larkin. What are you drinking?"

Larkin said, "This is business, Nick."

"For the squarehead too? He's not welcome here."

"Banjo's my deputy."

Diamond's arm was no longer in a sling, but there was a mark on his face that hadn't been there when Larkin had seen him last. Diamond must have guessed what was behind that quick appraisal, for he said, "We seem to be matched up evenly again. You're looking a little on the peaked side, though, Larkin. Just what can I do for you?"

"You can have this place closed by noon

to-morrow," Larkin said. "According to what the Boxed-C boys told me, there's a train out of here at one o'clock. Be on it, Nick. You and all your crew."

"Does that go for the rest of Santone Street, or just for the Fandango?"

"I'm starting here, Nick. I know this place is run crooked. That marked deck proved it. I'll look into the others later. I'm playing no favourites."

The piano crashed out a discordant fanfare; the curtains of the little stage were parting jerkily, and a blast of applause went up. From the corner of his eye Larkin saw Melody on the stage; she was wearing that same gown she'd worn the night she'd waited for him in the livery stable. She began singing, her voice soft and low and plaintive, and Diamond said, "How do you like her, Larkin?"

The question was too pointed, too incongruous at a time like this, and Larkin smelled a trap in it. He shrugged and said, "Who is she?"

"It doesn't matter," Diamond said, but his eyes never left Larkin's face. "Tell me this, Larkin: just what are you getting out of the deal?"

"A marshal's pay, Nick."

Diamond took on the look of a man witnessing something that defied the laws of nature; it was always like this with the Nick Diamonds; they measured others with their own yardstick and were lost when it failed to give them a tally they could understand. Diamond said, "I offered you better than that. And you threw me out of a window for making the bid."

Anger tugged at Larkin, but he put his mind against it. He said, "You made one mistake, Nick. One bad mistake. You shouldn't have tried running me out of town. Half an hour more and I'd have been gone, anyway. For keeps. But you couldn't wait." He backed away. "Come on, Banjo," he said. "Remember, Nick, to-morrow noon's the deadline."

Outside, Sorenson said, "You didn't ask 'em about the spurs!"

Larkin raised his hand to the other's shoulder; there was sympathy in that gesture, and a certain futility, too. He said, "If we'd asked, we'd only have put them wise. Maybe your man will be leaving town to-morrow. That can't be helped. But maybe they'll all choose to stay. You'll have your hour then."

Sorenson said, "Goot . . . goot . . ." And Larkin smiled, knowing then that he'd made no mistake. . . .

At deep dusk Larkin came to the big frame house of Sheldon Abbott and mounted to the porch and knocked upon the door, and it was Amy who admitted him. Her handshake was quick and perfunctory, her greeting couched in the accepted phrases, and she took his sombrero and gunbelt and stowed these away and then quickly led him to where Abbott waited in his wheel-chair in the living-room. From the doorway Larkin saw the man, and his first thought was that Abbott had grown older than the years between warranted. Abbott smiled and extended his hand, but Larkin said with no animosity, "Are you sure you want it this way?"

Abbott said, "We're not youngsters any more, Dave. Whatever passed between us long ago is long ago forgotten. I'm sorry I couldn't come out to the ranch to see you this past week."

"I'd meant to ride that way again," Amy said quickly. "But the days flew too fast for me."

Larkin thought, *You'd have come, yes, if he'd let you.* He had already read the possessive jealousy of the man, but he crossed the room and took Abbott's hand. Amy said, "Dinner is ready to serve," and she got behind Abbott's wheel-chair and shoved it into the adjoining dining-room. A linen covering made a long table seem vaster; candlelight caught the glint of properly placed silverware and fragile china; and Amy said, "You sit at the far end, Dave, opposite to Sheldon." She moved to a chair between them, and Larkin hastily withdrew the chair for her and caught the quizzical arch of Abbott's eyebrows, the man's faint smile of amusement.

That was the beginning, and after an Indian woman began silently serving them, they made light talk, and Larkin found himself mouthing the usual things and growing increasingly uncomfortable. At first that baffled him; it was not because these two were working so hard at being charming, nor that he was too mindful of the queerness of the relationship among them. It went deeper than that, and suddenly he sensed the truth, for he had eaten this dinner many times in many towns. There'd been candlelight before, and white linen, and silverware treasured from generation to generation, and hosts and hostesses who made small and polite talk while he shared their table.

That was it. There was this breed of people; they came from another world, and they brought their way of living with them to the far frontiers. They were the builders; perhaps they never turned their hand to hammer or saw, yet they built an ancient culture upon a newer, cruder foundation. They were respectability; they shuddered at the sight of

172

death, and they deplored the mud and dust and sweat and profanity and blood that went into the winning of this virgin land. And so they fed the Dave Larkins.

He closed his eyes, and he saw how it would be at noon to-morrow; the guns would blare when Diamond refused to leave, and the Diamonds always refused to leave. There would be the heavy smell of powder-smoke, and men beating their heels in the death tattoo against the floor of the Fandango, or falling into the dust of Santone Street to writhe away their lives. But that had to be, too; that had to come so that respectability could stay reared upon that new and crude foundation, and that was why Dave Larkin was needed, and that was why he sat at such a table, accepted and yet an alien.

Yes, that was the way of it. They gave him a badge and that made him different than the other men with guns; a piece of tin justified his brand of killing, and when he'd made the town safe for them, they would not be without gratitude. They would keep him here if he chose to stay; they would build his legend with retelling, and some day, perhaps, they'd even put up a monument to him on a street that was staid and quiet. They would honour him, just as they were doing to-night, yet they would stand apart from him, looking at him

173

from the corners of their eyes, respecting him and being in awe of him, yet letting him know that he wasn't their breed, though he was necessary to them.

All this he saw, and it took the taste from his food, and he knew now why he had put his guns away and turned his back upon the profession of his choosing. And yet he also knew why he had belted on those guns again; this thing that this kind of people reared upon the prairie was a good thing, and he must help sustain it. There was Jimmy Davis to remember.

Amy said suddenly, "Dave! Are you ill? From the look of you I'd say the doctor let you out of bed too soon!"

Her voice recalled him to reality; he glanced at her, and for a fleeting moment saw her as the girl he'd known and gone riding with across Boxed-C's moonlit acres. But she was wearing this low-cut gown she'd worn the night she'd come to his room in the Amarillo House; she was like something carved from ivory in the candlelight; she was Mrs. Sheldon Abbott to the tips of her finger-nails to-night, and the illusion was quickly lost.

Without answering her, he looked at Sheldon Abbott and said, "Matt Hobbs tells me you'll have to confirm my appointment as marshal."

"Of course," Abbott said. "That's already done. I signed the paper this afternoon. Didn't Matt tell you? I asked you here to-night to renew an old acquaintance — and to inquire about your plans."

Larkin said, "I was in the Fandango this afternoon. I've given Diamond until to-morrow at twelve to be gone."

Abbott frowned. "You're abrupt, I'll concede. But do you think that that was wise?"

"I've seen these towns before," Larkin said. "Look hard, and you'll always find that there's one place that's the core of everything that's wrong. There may be other saloons on Santone Street that need closing, but you'll find them suddenly respectable once the Fandango's been padlocked."

Abbott said, "I'd hoped you'd take this job, Larkin. Gun-handy gents come a dime a dozen; I wanted a man with brains enough to be discreet. Swayback serves a pretty wide swath of range; the pay of the ranches is spent here. A cowboy on town night doesn't want the kind of fun he finds north of the tracks. If the lid is clamped down too tightly here, he'll take his money to some other town. I thought you'd understand that I wanted Swayback respectable, but not as respectable as a corpse."

The napkin had been a nuisance to Larkin;

he balled it in his fist and put it beside his plate. He said, "Nick Diamond happens to be a friend of King Conover. That surprises you, eh? But that doesn't change anything, anyway. I can't kill half a snake, Abbott. And I can't kill him according to somebody else's directions. Do you want the badge back?"

Amy said faintly, "There's no need for anger, Dave!"

He looked at her and was sorry for his outburst; whatever else she might be, she was Cultus Pierce's daughter, and he knew that that half of her blood must count too.

Abbott said, "No, there's no call for anger." But he'd half-risen from his wheel-chair, and even though he settled back abruptly, Larkin's suspicion was born at that moment.

"Go and sleep on this man," Abbott advised. "You'll see it my way. A good scare will make Diamond conduct his place properly. Maybe you've already given him that."

Larkin came to a stand. "I've enjoyed the dinner," he said. "I'll be on my way now. But we might as well have this straight between us, Abbott. If I wear the badge, I do my own thinking."

Amy saw him to the door; he collected his sombrero and gun-belt and gave her his hand, and she looked very small and very frightened. She said, "Good night, Dave. Please think over what he's said. He wants whatever is best for Swayback; the question is which one of you sees the clearer."

He said, "Good night, Amy," and there was no promise in it.

Outside, he crossed over to that big cottonwood where Melody had stood a week before. Pausing here, he reached a decision, and he shaped up a cigarette and hid the match's quick flare behind his hand, and was careful afterwards to keep the glow of the cigarette from showing. In this way he began a vigil that was prompted only by that merest shadow of suspicion. Yet he kept remembering Abbott half-rising from the wheel-chair, and he had to know if any part of the man's paralysis was feigned.

He was sorry now that anger had driven him to leave so abruptly; it would have been better to have stayed inside to watch Abbott; now he could only wait and count on luck. He had learned patience long ago, but it was an endless hour before the lights winked from the first to the second storey, and he saw a shade drawn on one of the upper windows and glimpsed Amy's swiftly-moving silhouette. That would be her bedroom, but how could Abbott manoeuvre his wheel-chair to the second storey? So wondering, he saw a light blossom on the ground floor, to the side of the house, and Larkin moved swiftly then, putting himself at an angle where he could watch the window, yet keeping at a good distance from the house.

Abbott wheeled his chair to the window, got a hold on the shade and drew it down. The man was apparently capable of undressing himself and getting from the chair to the bed, and Larkin put his careful speculation on that. He knew little of paralysis; the sum of his knowledge being that a man usually recovered from it gradually. But if Abbott were completely cured and was feigning incapacity . . . ?

Twenty minutes later the window of Abbott's room blacked out, but still Larkin stood; he had hoped to see the man's silhouette against the shade, and if Abbott were standing, his suspicion would have been confirmed. But Abbott had obviously retired, the vigil had been in vain, and Larkin was about to turn away when he heard the clip-clop of hoofs as a rider came walking his horse towards the house. That rider had come from the prairie beyond the town; he stopped his mount at a distance from the house and swung from the saddle and left the horse anchored by trailing reins and went stealthily to the picket fence surrounding the yard and quickly clambered over it. Larkin glanced upwards at

Amy's window; it, too, was black. The house lay swathed in darkness, and a man was creeping towards Abbott's window.

Tense with interest, Larkin moved out from the shadow of a tree, regretted his action and stepped back again. Starlight gave him a murky glimpse of the man, and he saw that the fellow was at Abbott's window and was tapping lightly, and now the window was being raised an inch or two from the inside. The man began talking in a low voice that failed to carry with coherence to Larkin; he saw the fellow gesticulating, and ten minutes later the window was closed and the man crept back to his horse. Mounted, he began walking the animal out of town, but by then Larkin was running towards the main street, and when he came to the first establishment with a hitch-rail, he helped himself to the racked saddler that looked the speediest.

When he'd spun the horse about and come galloping back past Abbott's house and beyond the town to the dimness of the prairie, he thought at first that he'd lost his man. Then he made out vague movement ahead, and he belaboured the horse with his heels and wished mightily for spurs, but the distance was shortening between them.

The man ahead cast one backward glance and sensed pursuit, for starlight put a sheen on his drawn gun. It blossomed redly, and Larkin felt the breath of the bullet past his cheek. He wanted this man alive, but he dragged his own right-hand gun from its holster and fired; there was no choice now. He had that direction-sense of a natural gunfighter, the instinct that makes for good shooting, but the pitch of the saddle threw him off his aim. He saw the man ahead cast his hands upwards and come falling from the horse, and when he rode up to where the fellow lay, Larkin knew before he dismounted that the man was dead.

Turning the fellow over, Larkin thumbed a match to life and had his look, and the match burned down to his fingers before he remembered to cast it aside. He had seen this face before; he had seen it among the outlaws who followed King Conover and who had been upon that ledge high in the Silver Belts when Larkin had studied the group from inside the cave's mouth.

This much he knew for sure.

CHAPTER XI

When mid-evening brought an increased tempo of trade to the Fandango, Nick Diamond followed his usual ritual of inspection, surveying the liquor stocks, having a word or two with his house-men and with the half-dozen gun-hung gentry who were kept posted about the place as an insurance against trouble. Also he checked the tills to make sure there was change enough, and while he was doing this, one of the bartenders said, "Our last night, boss?"

Diamond gave him a sharp look, and, seeing a genuine worry and a loss of surety that was foreign to the man, Diamond smiled his smile and said, "They come and they go, these lawmen. Take a drink on the house, Mike. You're spooking at shadows."

Kinsella came to him in his own noiseless way and said, "She's still up there in her room, Nick. It'll take an hour at least before there's trade enough to bring her to the stage. Now?"

Diamond's eyes darkened; there was about him the look of a man who'd postponed an ugly task until a last moment, and, facing that moment, wished for another way. "O.K.," he said. "Lay it on thick — but not too thick. She's no fool."

Kinsella drew a savage satisfaction from the signs of Diamond's regret. "Interested in a little side bet?" he asked. "A hundred bucks says she goes out of here as soon as we finish our spiel."

Anger seized Diamond. "Damn you, no! Do you think I'm finding any fun in this?"

Kinsella said softly, "And you told me once to keep my hands off her!"

"Come on," Diamond said.

Together they climbed the stairs, and Diamond let them into his office. The lamp hung just above his desk; he got it aglow and the light revealed a scattering of chairs and a low horse-hair couch upon which Diamond sometimes slept. The lamp adjusted, Diamond cleared his throat, winked at Kinsella and said, "You look worried, Sig. To-morrow's just another day. And think of the surprise Dave Larkin's going to get."

They both heard the bed springs creak faintly in the room beyond. Kinsella began a silent padding about the room, and he pointed to the knothole with a long finger. "You're pinning a lot of faith in King Conover, Nick. Sure, he's anxious to get his kid brother out of jail, and him hitting the town early to-morrow morning will keep Larkin and Hobbs and Sorenson mighty busy. But supposing Larkin's lucky enough to still be alive at noon? He won't go chasing Conover back into the hills. He'll be down here closing up the Fandango."

Diamond laughed. "Pour yourself a drink, Sig. Conover's been hating Dave Larkin ever since Larkin slipped through his fingers. I've got a ten-spot that says Larkin will be dead before the first sidewalk is swept off to-morrow morning."

"I'll take that drink, Nick. But not the bet. I still ain't sure it's all gonna work out like you think."

Kinsella took a bottle from Diamond's desk, found a glass and sloshed whisky into it and downed the stuff. Diamond began humming softly, the song aimless and care-free, but his eyes had no light in them, and his face had hardened. Beyond, the bed springs had creaked again; shortly thereafter the door of Melody's room softly opened and closed; they heard her footsteps fade away towards the stairs, and Kinsella said exultantly, "She's gone, Nick!" Then anger put an edge to his voice. "You didn't want to find out the truth, did you? Your idea was to give her rope enough to hang herself, but it's our twine that's likely to be tangled. We gave her half a truth, and she'll carry it to Larkin. But when Conover doesn't show up at the crack of dawn,

Larkin will keep waiting for him. And Conover will ride in at high noon!"

"Larkin's talking business with Sheldon Abbott tonight," Diamond said. "She won't get word to him. Now get after her, Sig. See where she goes, and what she tells. Then come back here."

Kinsella said, "God, Nick! Does she have to tie the rope around *your* neck before you'll see the truth?"

Diamond came to a stand behind the desk. He said flatly, harshly, "You're getting too big for the size of your britches, Sig. You still don't know but what she's gone out for a breath of air."

"No?" said Kinsella, and grinned and glided from the room.

Melody came along Santone Street with her cloak flying behind her; she was dressed tonight as she'd been dressed when she'd waited for Dave Larkin in Santone's livery stable. She jostled men aside in her wild haste, and she almost stumbled when she came to the dark region of the tracks that divided the town. This time she had no trouble locating the big building that housed the town's officials, but when she came into the main corridor, the heels of her slippers raising clamorous echoes, she again found most of the flanking doors shut, but there was lamplight beyond the open doorway leading into Judge Bragg's chambers. The old gentleman sat dozing behind his desk, but he awoke as she came hurrying up the aisle. That broken window still hadn't been replaced; the burlap sack lifted lazily with the breeze.

Bragg said, "Good evening, miss."

Breathlessly, Melody said, "Larkin? Mr. Larkin? Where is he?"

Her desperate urgency took the last of the sleep out of Bragg; she could see that. "Larkin, miss, is taking supper with the mayor."

"Will you fetch him here? I haven't much time!"

"Now, miss, you don't go taking the town marshal away from the mayor's table," he said placatingly. "What is it that's disturbing you?"

Once before, on that night when she'd learned that Larkin was a prisoner in the Silver Belts, she'd been tempted to tell Bragg the truth; instead she'd gone to Amy Abbott for help. Now she made a quick decision and said, "There's no time to explain everything. King Conover is hitting this town at dawn to get his brother out of jail. Nick Diamond is counting on Larkin dying during that raid. Now will you have Larkin fetched here?"

Bragg was all attention. Sitting here at his

185

desk, a man aloof from the town's activity, he had had many pieces of a pattern placed before him this past week or so, and he had fitted these pieces together, taking a delight in the game. Now he said with unerring instinct, "You learned this at the Fandango, of course. I've suspected an alliance between Nick Diamond and King Conover. Hobbs hasn't been around all evening, which means he'll be hard to find. Yes, miss, I'll get word to Larkin. You can be sure of that."

She said, "Do you suppose there's still time? If Conover's hitting the town at daybreak, he'll be leaving Big Baldy some time during the night."

"Big Baldy!" Bragg ejaculated, and now the map he'd built from Larkin's delirium-tinged knowledge made sense.

"Yes, Big Baldy. That's where Sig Kinsella rode when he went to see Conover on business for Nick Diamond. Yes, I learned all this at the Fandango. I work there, but I'll be leaving after to-night. No, there's no need to worry about me. Judge, if someone rode fast now, they might get to the Silver Belts in time to head off Conover's men! There's a chance, isn't there?"

He said, "I'll get word to Larkin, miss."

"But supposing he's left Abbott's? Supposing you can't find him?"

He saw then what she was suggesting, and he said with utter amazement, "Miss, you're meaning for *me* to ride to the hills?"

She said, "There's a dozen places where one man could fort up and keep Conover bottled for hours. I've heard whisky talk of you in the Fandango, Judge. They say you were partner to such men as Wyatt Earp and Bat Masterson. They tell that you served under Custer. Why, I've even heard that Billy the Kid once backed down from you, Judge. Lies — all of them?"

He regarded his expansive stomach and sighed a long and regretful sigh. "The boldness of youth," he said. "I'm an old man now."

"Didn't I see a horse at the hitch-rack outside? Yours, Judge? Can I have the use of him?"

He came to a stand then; about him there was the look of eagles, and she could believe, now, every tale that had been tagged to his name. He said, "You are a brave girl, miss — so brave that you shame me. Yo' job is to get yourself out of sight. After to-morrow there'll be no Fandango, but until then you may be in danger. I'll go now to Sheldon Abbott's to talk to Larkin."

"But if you miss him?"

"If I miss him? Then I shall ride to the hills

— alone, if necessary. I'm not without knowledge of King Conover's hideout. There'll be no rain at dawn."

Melody said, "Thank you! Oh, thank you!" Turning, she ran out of the room and along the corridor. Not until she was outside the building did she realise that there was no need to hurry now, no destination for her. All that she would ever do in Swayback had been done. Remembering this, she knew an old loneliness, an old feeling of being without roots. From here on there would be sooty trains, or stagecoaches creaking over rutted roads, other towns and other honkytonks, old songs and new faces — and the remembrance of something left behind.

That was her destiny; that had always been her destiny; the pattern in Swayback had varied only that she'd helped two men. There was Banjo Sorenson and the deck of marked cards that had saved him from trouble, and there was Dave Larkin, whose life had become interwoven with hers because he'd taken that deck and used it according to her wish. Yet that was finished, too. Both of these men belonged to something else — one to a love that was hopeless and abiding, one to a hate that closed his heart to all else.

She had Bragg's solemn promise that all that could be done to stop King Conover would be done, and she believed Bragg. There was nothing more.

If a man lingered in the shadows that banked beside the building, lingered there beneath the one lighted window, she didn't see him. She turned southwards and came across the tracks again; she was headed for the Fandango this one last time; she had her clothes to get, and her savings; they were in that room of hers. After that . . .

She knew, suddenly, that she wouldn't leave. Not until another sundown. She had to see the sequel to all this; she had to know what the morrow brought to Dave Larkin; but she'd move out of the Fandango first.

And so she came back to Santone Street, hurrying again, knowing that very shortly she'd be expected to make her first appearance of the night on that little stage, and knowing also that she must be into the Fandango and out again before Nick Diamond came to her room to see what was delaying her. But before she reached the saloon, she had to pass the dark, closed doorway of the livery stable, and here, in this empty, silent section of the street, a man stepped out to block the way. She almost screamed, realising only then how taut her nerves had become. But Banjo Sorenson said soothingly, "I didn't mean to scare you, miss."

She said, "Oh — you . . . !" and would have fallen except that he caught her. He was thrusting something into her hand; it glinted dully in the starlight, and she saw that it was the spur he'd been showing to the little boys that other night. He said, "You seen this before, huh?"

She almost dropped it; and something crossed his broad, bovine face, erasing the boyishness. He said, "I keeped remembering how scared you got when you saw this spur the other night. I keeped t'inking maybe you could tell me who had it in the Fandango. I got to know."

She said, "What is this to you?"

"He killed Greta," he said slowly. "He killed my sister and busted his spur while he was fighting with her. That's why I got deputy badge from Larkin. But to-morrow, maybe, we chase 'em all avay, and I never find *him*. You got to tell me vich one!"

She saw it all now; she understood the hate that had driven him, and all of her pity came welling, and she could have named his man for him. But the vague fear that had made Joshua Bragg want to banish this giant from Swayback for Sorenson's own safety was a real fear to her. She thought: *Yes, I can tell him! And he'll go in there and get himself killed, and I'll have that to remember always — that it*

190

was a word from me that sent him to his death!

She clutched at his shirt, and she said, "Banjo, you like me. I've seen it in your eyes as you watched me sing. Will you marry me? To-night?"

Bewilderment clouded his face — that, and the beginning of anger. He said, "You yoost makin' crazy talk. You trying to take my mind avay from what I've been saying."

Her voice sounding hysterical in her ears, she said, "I'm leaving the Fandango to-night. There'll be no job for me after to-morrow, anyway. I'm riding out of town as soon as I get my things. Ride with me, Banjo. If we can't find Judge Bragg at his office, we'll be married in the next town."

His fingers closed on her arm, hurting her. *"Who vore the spurs?"*

"He's gone, Banjo. He was some saddle-bum who wanted to trade those broken spurs for a drink. The apron felt sorry for him and made the swap. He came and went long ago."

"Vich way did he go?"

"I don't know!" she cried. "And I've got to hurry now. Are you riding with me, Banjo?"

He gave this his solemn consideration; his eyes searched her face, and she tried desperately to make it so he'd read truth there. She saw him turn humble, and she knew that she had won. But, "I ban mighty proud to be asked," he said. "But I got deputy job to do for Dave Larkin to-morrow."

She said, "He won't care. Don't you see — he must have given you the badge because he felt sorry for you, knowing how much you hated the Fandango. He wanted you to be able to remember that you were in on the finish. But he doesn't need you, really. He'll have Matt Hobbs behind him — and half the town, if I can believe saloon talk. Why, you haven't even worn a gun, up until lately. Now will you wait here till I get my things?"

He drew her to him and kissed her awkwardly; the touch of him left her unmoved, but she thought: *I can learn to love him. I WILL learn to love him. He's a boy, and he'll always be a boy, and I'll spend my days mothering him. But when the hate is washed away there'll be nothing in him but kindness, and he'll spend it on me. At least I'll never walk with loneliness again.*

Banjo said, "I'll be vaiting."

She hurried away from him; there was a rear door to the Fandango and she used it, coming unobtrusively into the vast, smoky room. She saw Nick Diamond talking to one of the bartenders; Sig Kinsella was not within her range of vision, and she ran quickly up the stairs and to her room. Her telescope was under the bed; she got it out and tugged at the straps and began emptying drawers into it. Her savings, turned into currency, were tucked under the mattress, and she got the money and dropped it into the front of her dress. She wondered if she should change to clothes for the trail and decided not to risk the time. And she was strapping the telescope when the door opened and Sig Kinsella stepped inside and closed the door and put his back to it.

She came to her feet with a quick intake of her breath, and fear was in her eyes. He smiled and said, "You weren't leaving without saying good-bye, were you?" She knew this to be a cat-and-mouse play, so she made no answer.

Anger brightened his eyes, and he came towards her and got a hold on her arm and twisted it. He said, "You little she-Judas! That show of innocence fooled the boss, but it never fooled me! Not for a minute. So you went straight to Judge Bragg with your story, eh? I was standing outside that broken window listening to every word that was said. Bragg took one look at that pretty face of yours and decided he was still young enough to play at being a man. He made you a lot of fancy talk — big talk about what he was going to do, but he was still in his office ten minutes after you'd left. From all the sound he was making, I'd say he hadn't left his desk. He got short on guts when he started thinking over what he'd promised to do."

She didn't want to believe this; she'd pinned too much faith in Bragg, and suddenly her own fear was gone and in its place was a fear for Dave Larkin. She said, "Bragg may not ride to the hills himself. I was foolish to expect that, I suppose. But he'll get word to Larkin just the same."

"And a lot of good it will do. Everything Nick and me talked about was for you to hear. Sure, Conover's coming — but not until high noon to-morrow. By then Larkin will have figured that the talk you heard was crazy, and he'll be heading for Santone Street. Either that or he'll be off in the hills on a wild-goose chase."

He drew her hard against him, still keeping his grip on her arm, and he got his free arm around her and pinioned her close. She could smell the reek of his breath, and she felt the stubble of his chin rasp against her cheek, and the anger and hatred in him was replaced by another emotion, and, reading it in his eyes, she began fighting at him with all the strength she possessed. But she knew she was no match for him, and she was sobbing when his grip was broken and he was wrenched around by

194

a ponderous hand placed upon his shoulder. Only then did she realise that the door had opened and that Banjo Sorenson was in the room.

He brought Kinsella spinning around; the Swede's face was livid, and Kinsella, seeing that murderous anger, dropped his hand towards his thigh, but Melody was quicker. She snatched the gun from Kinsella's holster and flung it towards the bed, and Sorenson said then, incongruously, "I got t'inking you was taking awfully long time getting back, so I come."

She said faintly, "I'm glad you did!"

Kinsella, without his gun, was drained of courage; he took two slow backward steps away from Sorenson, his hands raised to ward off the Swede's threatening fists, and Kinsella said, "Now wait a minute! You've got no fight to make with me, Banjo!"

Sorenson said woodenly, "You ban no goot! You shoot that little boy, and now I catch you roughing up a girl. I ban gonna give you goot beating!"

Kinsella said, "Easy with those big fists! The girl isn't worth fighting for. She doesn't give a hoot for you. She's crazy about Dave Larkin. Give me time and I'll prove it. And shooting the kid was an accident. He was just a thieving little rat anyway. Only a couple of days before that ruckus, he sneaked in here and swiped a pair of spurs from my room."

Only now did Kinsella realize he had made a grave mistake. Even then there could have been no knowledge in him of how he'd betrayed himself; he hadn't known of the search Sorenson had made for the owner of those spurs. But Sorenson's face must have given him warning; Sorenson's eyes had widened, and his mouth dropped open, and he looked like nothing human. Sorenson spoke, but it was a guttural ejaculation in his own tongue. He came lunging forward with his hands outspread, and Melody knew she was going to witness murder.

Then she saw Nick Diamond; and she was the only one who saw him. He had framed himself in the open doorway behind Sorenson; he had taken one quick look, and his hand was going under his coat, and when it darted into view again he was raising a gun aloft. He brought it down across Sorenson's skull; Melody's anguished cry of warning was lost in the thud of that blow, and Sorenson's knees unhinged and his eyes rolled upwards, and he crashed to the floor, falling across the packed telescope.

Kinsella found his voice. He said hoarsely, "I was never gladder to see you, Nick!"

Diamond said, "I saw the Swede climbing

the stairs." His glance moved to Melody. "What did you find out, Sig?"

"She went to Judge Bragg, Nick. She told him what she'd heard here. He won't be doing much about it, though."

Diamond's eyes dropped, and it took him a moment to speak. "Sorenson is Larkin's deputy," he said then. "And she's the girl who's been spying for him. You win there, Sig. But it all adds up to the fact that both of them must mean something to him. We'll have them here in the Fandango when he comes to close us at noon. Maybe that will slow him a little. Tie them both up, Sig, and we'll lock them in this room. Here, I'll lend you a hand."

No, Judge Bragg hadn't gone to the house of Sheldon Abbott. Long after Melody had left him, he continued to sit at his desk, remembering his promise to her — the pledge that he would either get word to Dave Larkin of King Conover's impending raid, or that he, himself, would ride to the hills in an effort to checkmate Conover. Already he had come to regret that promise; it had been inspired by Melody's display of courage, and by his own sense of unworthiness — and by a secret knowledge of himself which he had shared with no man in Swayback.

That knowledge stretched back over the past thirty years of his life, and as he sat here dreaming, he saw those years again. Beyond the broken window, Sig Kinsella was at that moment loitering, waiting for any sound of Bragg's departure, but the judge didn't know that, and he had grown oblivious of time. He was lost in reverie; he was back once more in a tiny cross-roads store in the Montana badlands to the north and east of here.

It had been his store, that little log and frame structure not far from the banks of the Missouri. There had been a sign outside that proclaimed it his, but the sign had faded with the years and he'd never bothered to have it re-lettered. He remembered the store almost regretfully now; it had been a haven against the strife of a peopled world; it had smelled of merchandise that ranged from a bar of soap to a silver-encrusted saddle, and he had loved it and hated it. For there he had lived alone, and the world had swung past his door, and he had bought security at the price of monotony.

Yes, that was it — but he'd come to find it a bad bargain. He'd served trappers in the earlier days, and steamboat men, and he'd seen the longhorn come to Montana, and he'd weathered the hard winter that had changed all cattledom and brought a better breed of stock to the tawny hills. He'd listened to the tales of men who'd ranged from the Rio to the Yukon; outlaws had eaten tomatoes from cans purchased from his stock; sabre-clanking cavalrymen had requisitioned supplies from him; silent riders with the dust of far trails had leaned against his counter. He'd lived the second-hand adventures of such men, but his own world had been changeless and limited and infinitely dull.

He could speak of men like Custer and Earp and Hickok and Billy the Kid — and with reasonable accuracy; he had known men who'd brushed elbows with the great; for those men had been his customers. And, listening to them, he had felt a growing dissatisfaction; the years were running away from him, and nothing changed — the seasons made their swing, and he grew older and paunchier, and adventure passed him by.

And so he'd awakened one morning to the realisation that nothing chained him here to an existence that had become intolerable — nothing but himself. He'd sold the store then, sold it to a New Englander with a bad set of lungs and a thick roll of currency, sold everything but his Sunday clothes and a treasured walking-stick, and a mule. And with these he had set forth, an old man in search of his own queer kind of Fountain of Youth.

He had come to Swayback merely because it had lain across his trail; he had liked the town for its gusto and its promise of growth. He had been accepted, and he might have assumed any personality, for he had dozens to choose from. He was a man re-born, and that gave him a sense of shaping his own destiny, so he donned dignity, tempered it with affability, gave it a dash of colour, and put himself in the town hall. He talked well, and his talk went the rounds of the town, and he came to be known as a man of parts, an associate of the great. Until to-night no one had ever challenged the tales he'd told; Melody had been the first to hint that they were lies.

Lies . . . ? Combing his skimpy goatee with his fingers, he wondered if he'd finally made himself believe in the legend of his own creation — the legend of Joshua X. Bragg. Yet here was the test, and he flinched from it, though at the same time he was tempted. Keep King Conover pinned in the hills? It could be done, perhaps. One man could do it alone — one man with the proper knowledge and the proper ingenuity — and courage. He placed the map before him, the map he'd made after Dave Larkin had described the canyon hideout. That hideout was on the face of Big Baldy; Melody had supplied the missing piece that completed his information. The story was here for the reading; the strength and the weakness of King Conover's lair was obvious. The bridge was the key.

Destroy that suspension bridge across the gorge and you still hadn't checkmated Conover. No, Conover could go back through the cave, just as Larkin had done, and come down the other side of Big Baldy and eventually reach the horses in the corral that was on the opposite side of the gorge from the cave. But if that bridge were destroyed, say by midnight, Conover would have to waste hours in reaching the corral. Destroy the bridge, and

Conover would not raid Swayback at the crack of dawn.

It was as simple as that, and therein lay Joshua Bragg's temptation. One real adventure for the man whose adventures had all been borrowed from his betters. One actuality to balance against the tall tales he'd spun. After to-night's work, they'd speak of Judge Joshua Bragg with a respect untinged by any fleeting doubt. Even if he died at doing this, they'd still remember.

He was not of the stuff of martyrs, and he quickly dismissed this last thought. He turned his mind to Swayback, and it came to him that this would be a great thing he would be doing for the town. Swayback had taken him in and accepted him and put its trust in him, asking little in return. Swayback was *his* town, and King Conover would ride to bring death to its streets.

So thinking, he carefully hooked his walking-stick over his arm, blew out the lamp on his desk, locked his chambers and groped out of the building. His horse was at the hitch-rack; he'd long since learned that a mule was not the mount expected of the town's justice. Astride the horse, he headed towards Sheldon Abbott's, but even at a distance he could see that the house was dark, though the hour was still reasonably early. Dave Larkin must have departed immediately after supper, and the Abbotts had then retired. Turning, Bragg headed back towards the busier part of Swayback's main street, and it occurred to him then that he didn't know where Larkin had taken quarters.

Remembering Matt Hobbs, he wanted mightily to consult the man, to tell Hobbs what was in the wind and to seek his counsel. This was a reversal of the many times Hobbs had come to him for help, but he sensed the difference and it shamed him. Hobbs had wanted only advice; Joshua Bragg was hoping to borrow courage from a braver man.

His eyes swept the street; most of the establishments were still lighted. Perhaps a pinochle game was occupying Hobbs in the rear of the mercantile store; then, again, Hobbs and Dave Larkin and Banjo Sorenson might be prowling Santone Street to-night, feeling the temper of that part of town on the eve of the deadline Larkin had established for the Fandango. Likely it would take precious time to hunt them down, and it was many miles to that bridge on the slope of Big Baldy. He thought of leaving a note for Hobbs at the town hall, a note explaining his mission, but a feeling of urgency had begun to grow upon him, and he decided against wasting the time. Squaring his shoulders, Bragg jogged his mount into motion and picked his way between buildings, heading for the prairie beyond.

If he'd chosen a different direction and passed the darkened house of Sheldon Abbott, he might have found Dave Larkin loitering in the shadows. Or if there'd been moonlight, Bragg might have seen the man of King Conover's crew who came riding towards Swayback on a mysterious mission that involved the town's mayor. As it was, Bragg heard the stillness of the prairie night broken by the beat of hoofs off at a distance, but the starlight wasn't great enough to give him any real glimpse of the oncoming man, and the judge rode with no inkling of shaping events, skirting the Boxed-C an hour or so later as the moon rose.

Lights pin-pointed Pierce's ranch-house, and again Bragg was tempted, this time to take his tale to old Cultus and to get the Boxed-C crew at his back before riding on. Such a move could mean the end of King Conover; the Boxed-C had waited a long time for the chance Bragg could have now offered, but the risk was too great. A dozen men climbing Big Baldy, no matter how stealthily, would be sure to betray themselves; Conover, warned, might slip away from them, only to appear in Swayback at dawn. But *one* man with a plan and the courage might win through to checkmate the outlaw crew to-night.

Big Baldy was now looming above him, its crest spectral in its bareness by moonglow; Bragg lost himself in the chaos of timber and found a trail and began climbing. He was into unfamiliar country; he had ridden the range beyond Swayback many times, but he'd never ventured this deep into the hills. The sounds of the wooded night pecked at his nerves; he had known loneliness — thirty years of it — but there was a difference when a man found himself beyond sheltering walls. He almost despaired a dozen times and turned back, but he kept a spark of his courage alive, and he fanned it intermittently. And so he learned, in that long night's riding, the measure of his own manhood, for he did not fail Swayback, and he did not fail himself. And at last he heard the faint song of the creek that snaked along the gorge's bottom.

He was nearing the gorge, he knew, so he swung down stiffly from the saddle, tied his horse to a stout bush, hooked his walking-stick over his arm, and followed the trail on foot. Through the interlacing canopy of branches, he caught the glimmer of dying moonlight on the perpendicular face of the cliff rearing above the cave's mouth, and he sensed that this trail was likely to lead him directly to the bridge. He tasted triumph; luck had kept him on the right trail, and he had only to cut the ropes that held the bridge at this end. The whole structure would swing downwards, and King Conover would be delayed for half a day. It was midnight, he judged, and unless Conover had taken the trail, the victory was as good as ensured. It was as simple as that.

And then, from the brush that fringed this trail, someone said, "Just hoist your hands, feller, and stay rooted."

Bragg obeyed; the walking-stick clattered on the hard-packed trail, and he stood there with his hands raised, and the fear in him, and he was naked in his own eyes. He had thought this would be easy, and he had underestimated King Conover. He should have known that the outlaw, warned by the fact that Larkin had escaped with knowledge of the hideout, would have guards posted everywhere in anticipation of an attack by the ranchers of the flats. And seeing his own incompetence in matters such as these, he silently damned himself as an ancient fool who'd thought that an idea was armour enough for the storming of Conover's stronghold.

The guard came into view; he was short and burly and possessed of a face that was far from reassuring; he ran his hands over Bragg's clothing and said in vast astonishment, "No gun!"

Then he said, "Move along, mister!"

Bragg stooped and retrieved the walking-stick, a gesture that could have cost him his life, and then he was prodded forward. They came to the suspension bridge — another guard squatted here at its far end — and they crossed that swaying terror, all the emptiness beneath him putting a feathery feeling in Bragg's stomach, and they came to the ledge, an incongruous pair, the one wild and elemental and fitting into this stark and savage background, the other garbed in a jurist's staid black and carrying a fancy walking-stick as though he were strolling one of Swayback's most respectable streets.

The guard's shout fetched Conover out of the cave; others came tumbling after him, and someone kicked a fire to life on the ledge, and in this fitful light Conover pawed the sleep from his eyes and looked at his prisoner. He said "Search him," and he was obeyed, but the only thing approximating a weapon that was found was a huge jack-knife which Conover tossed over the lip of the ledge.

Then he said, "Tie him," and again he was obeyed. The walking-stick was wrenched away from Bragg; his hands were bound behind him, and his ankles were lashed, and he was dumped unceremoniously to hard seating upon the rock of the ledge. They stood ringed about him, this crew of Conover's, and King Conover said, "Now, just what fetched you here, mister?"

And thus did Joshua X. Bragg find himself with a second chance; he had bungled badly so far, and the fear was still in him, and he wanted to make wild denial of anything but the most innocent of motives. He wanted to say that he'd had no idea he was within miles of an outlaw hideout. He thought of claiming he'd gone for a moonlight ride into the hills and that his horse had thrown him and that he'd become lost, but he realised how ridiculous this would sound. He wanted to do anything that would take that baleful ring of eyes away from him, yet he wanted also to salvage something from the wreckage of his plan and his hopes.

That was why he said, "I came here, suh, to join up with you."

That brought him a chorus of heavy laughter, but none of it came from King Conover. His craggy face knotted by a frown, Conover said, "Join up with me! What kind of talk is this, you old fool?" He glanced at his men. "Do any of you know him?"

One spoke up, the one who'd once gone to Swayback to talk to Crad Conover through a cell window and who'd come back to the hills with the news of Dave Larkin's return. This fellow said, "He's Judge Bragg of the justice court. He's fairly new to the town, and he talks a big rep. I'd say to watch him, King. He's slyer than he looks."

Conover fastened his gaze upon Bragg again. "What's given you a taste for the owlhoot, Judge?"

"To-morrow, suh, theah's to be a showdown between Nick Diamond and the law of Swayback. You're involved, suh; you and Diamond have an alliance, and you'll be raiding Swayback to give Diamond a hand. Isn't that true, suh?"

Astonishment made Conover ludicrous. Kneeling, he got his fist in Bragg's vest and twisted hard, his face less than a foot from Bragg's. Conover said, "Larkin might have told you about me being teamed up with Nick. Larkin could have heard that, if he was only pretending to be unconscious when I first fetched him here. I've never been sure about that. *But how did you know I was raiding the town?*"

It was to Bragg's eternal glory that he could maintain dignity at a time like this. He said, "I, suh, manage to keep an ear to the ground. In my own interests, I assure you. I'm trading no information until I'm sure I'm accepted."

This sheer audacity staggered Conover as

209

nothing physical had ever done. He said hoarsely, "It's some kind of trick! Larkin's sent you here hoping you could fool me into talking. You've made a shot in the dark, and you want to know whether you've hit. Yes, I'm raiding Swayback to-morrow. But you won't be there to see it."

"I'd hoped I wouldn't be, suh," Bragg said blandly. "That's why I chose the dangers of the hills to-night in preference to the dangers of the town to-morrow."

Conover looked at his men again and said, "What the devil do you make of this jigger?" and that appeal was the admission of his own bewilderment.

Someone said, "Ask him what he figgered was in it for him, King."

Bragg managed a shrug. "I, suh, am fairly new to Swayback. But I know when a good thing has played itself out. Diamond will win to-morrow, with your help, suh. If it's to be Diamond's town by another sundown, I want to be with the winning side. Surely you can understand that, suh."

"Then why didn't you go to Diamond with your turncoat proposition?"

Bragg had anticipated that very question. "Because, suh, my one means of bargaining will interest you more than it will Diamond."

"Meaning?"

"A key, suh," said Bragg. "The key that unlocks Crad Conover's cell. Part of your plan, of course, must be to release yo' brother from jail. You can do that without my help, but the key will make it simpler."

"You were packing no key when we searched you. You're bluffing!"

"The key, suh, I hid down the trail — just before your man jumped me. Naturally, suh, I had no intention of putting it within your reach until you agreed to accept me."

Conover was thinking hard; Bragg could see the effort in the man's face, and Bragg congratulated himself then on his own careful manoeuvring of words. He had given himself a motive for being here; he had dangled a bit of bait before Conover's eyes, and he waited now for the yes or no that would mean Conover believed or disbelieved. But Conover said, "I could find out where you hid that key without promising you anything."

The way he said it put the feathery feeling back into Bragg's stomach; he wasn't sure whether he could stand torture, but he managed another shrug. "Why bother, suh? After all, I ask very little — merely that I be given protection when the bullets start buzzing tomorrow. And that after the powder-smoke settles, you and Diamond will remember who was yo' friend."

Conover gave that due consideration; the habitual wariness and the wild impatience that had warred within the man ever since Crad Conover's capture were again pulling at him. At last he said, "Fair enough. You're just a harmless old fool who wants to be on the right side of the fence. And you're smart enough to buy yourself in. Take me to the key."

Producing a knife, Conover slashed the bonds that held Bragg's wrists and ankles, and Bragg came to a stand, rubbing at his wrists and stamping circulation back into his feet. Then he set his hat at the proper angle, brushed himself carefully, picked up his walking-stick and started towards the bridge. "Come along, suh," he said, but Conover was already following him.

Bragg reached the bridge first; he paused here as though that swaying structure took a bit of courage for the crossing, and as he paused, he tugged at his walking-stick. The rumour of Swayback hadn't lied; there *was* a sword within the cane; it flashed brightly in the last of the moonlight, and it flicked out to sever one of the ropes that held the bridge.

This hadn't been the plan. Not at all. He'd hoped to cut the bridge at its other end, to pen the outlaws here on the ledge; cutting it in this manner meant that he'd be penned here with them. But he was afraid of that crossing, afraid that Conover would close the distance between them and be hard at his heels at the far end. As it was, Conover was coming towards him now with a wild bellow, just as Bragg cut the second rope. He was thinking then, was Bragg, what a tale this would make for the telling, but he knew that he would never live to do the telling. This was the choice he had made.

Something struck him along one side of his head, then; he never saw the gun that blossomed there on the ledge, nor knew which one of the outlaws had been the quickest of wit and trigger. As a black pool of darkness opened at his feet to swallow him, he only knew that he'd failed to completely destroy the bridge.

The day came to Swayback with the promise of a languid morning and a blazing afternoon; the peeping sun, thrusting lazily above the bluffs to the east, saw the sidewalks being swept, and there was much banging of shutters and creaking of pumps, and the greetings of one early riser to another, and the first clatter of dishes from the Chinaman's.

At eight o'clock, when Charlie Peters, the cashier, a grey and stooped little man, opened the bank, there were a few bonneted shoppers on that respectable street, and Peters had to tip his hat many times between the restaurant where he breakfasted and the building where he put in his day. At nine o'clock, when Abe Abercrombie, the bank president, a grey and pompous man, came to the bank, the street was alive with people. Thus was time marked in Swayback, and a man might have set his watch by the various manifestations of its passing. To-day's difference came from an acute awareness of Larkin's deadline for Nick Diamond, and the news had gotten around. There was none of your bantering among the loitering men, and there was much gazing to the south where Santone Street lay beyond the

214

railroad tracks. Swayback waited. Swayback held its breath and waited.

Matt Hobbs, limping into the marshal's office in the town hall at nine-fifteen, found Dave Larkin already there. Larkin lolled indolently in the swivel-chair behind the desk that had been Hobbs', a man without muscles or nerves, seemingly, but the marks of sleeplessness were upon Larkin, and these Hobbs was quick to see. Whereupon Hobbs said, "Ye look like ye've been wrestling with the devil."

Behind him Larkin had put a night of hating himself; he had lived long hours with the knowledge that he should have returned to the house of Sheldon Abbott, there to demand an explanation about a certain nocturnal visitor. But he hadn't. There was dirt under his finger-nails, for he'd commandeered a shovel and buried a man on the prairie — a man from the high hills — and bitterness had burned him since. There was a ceaseless refrain that still beat through his weary consciousness, an endless song that was always the same. *I can go to him and face him with the truth and tell him to be on that one o'clock train, along with Diamond. I can banish him, and the tale will follow after him to the ends of the frontier, but his infamy will stain her as well.* Such was the thought that had fettered him, and put the hell in his eyes.

Now he said, "We've got a great deal to do before high noon, Matt."

"Ye've a hundred men waiting for you to give them orders, if ye want them," Hobbs said.

"Diamond I'll handle alone, Matt. It's King Conover I'm worried about. I can't be on both sides of the railroad tracks at the same time."

Hobbs arched his tufted eyebrows. "Ye're remembering the talk ye heard between Conover and Sig Kinsella when ye were a prisoner on the ledge? The palaver about the bank and when would be the best time to hit at it?"

Larkin nodded. "We've kept what I heard on the ledge between ourselves, Matt. It's probably worried Diamond and Conover because they can't be sure that I know about their partnership."

"Judge Bragg suspected the truth," Hobbs said. "He guessed that the note Conover sent about swapping you for Crad was written by Diamond. Ye're thinking that Conover will strike at the bank some noon?"

"*This* noon," Larkin said.

That brought the surprise into Hobbs' eyes, and Larkin said, "One of Conover's men rode into town last night, Matt. I gave him a chase afterwards, and he's dead and buried. We know for sure that Diamond was doing Conover the favour of spying on the bank for the outlaw crew. Supposing Conover's figuring on doing a favour for Diamond in return? What better day than this one, then — when the law will be busy at the other end of town? And what else could have fetched one of Conover's men into town?"

Hobbs said, "You reckon I'd better get word to Abercrombie over at the bank?"

"You can do better than that, Matt. I'll be riding out of Swayback to-night. It will please me to leave you the kind of town you want, and to have King Conover salted away at the same time. Go to every man who's showed himself willing to back the law to-day. Tell them to keep their rifles handy, and to stay indoors. We'll set a trap, savvy. That trap will be sprung only when you give some kind of signal — three shots fired into the air, say. Maybe I'm guessing wrong, and Conover won't show up. The fact that his man didn't return to the hills last night may make him skittish. But if he isn't here at high noon, I'll be going down to Santone Street. Alone. You stay posted here where you can keep an eye on this street and the bank."

Hobbs said, "I'll be going now to spread the word among the boys."

At the doorway he hesitated. "Have ye seen Judge Bragg this morning, Dave? He weren't at the Chinaman's at breakfast time, and he weren't in his chambers when I came down the hall a few minutes ago."

Larkin shook his head, and Hobbs said, "He talks a mighty stout heart, does Bragg, but I've wondered at times how much truth there is in him. Do ye suppose he's smelled big trouble and skinned out?"

He sighed a heavy sigh, and in it was a genuine regret and a grave disappointment. Larkin said, "Many a man who makes smoky talk can't stand the smell of the real stuff in his nostrils, Matt. Don't take it too hard about Bragg. Me, I'm wondering what's keeping Banjo Sorenson this morning."

Hobbs vanished then, leaving Larkin to his own thoughts, and it was well past ten when the ex-marshal put in another appearance. He found Larkin in the same indolent posture, but there was this difference: Larkin was cleaning his guns. He reassembled one of the forty-fives as Hobbs made a report, took an experimental look along the sights, spun the cylinder carefully and dumped the weapon into its holster.

Hobbs said, "Every merchant has got a rifle or a scatter-gun behind his counter this morning. Every window's got a pair of eyes behind it, watching the street. The trap is set and ready to snap, Dave."

Larkin said, "If they come, let them get as

far as the bank. Let them even get inside and out again. That will be their weakest moment, when some are with the horses and some are loaded down with loot. There'll never be another chance to bag Conover like this one."

Hobbs said, "Have ye seen Bragg yet?"

"No, nor Sorenson. I can't savvy what's keeping him. The Swede didn't run."

Hobbs sighed his heavy sigh again, then shook his head, a man dismissing an unworthy thought. "I'll be getting over to the Chinaman's shortly. 'Tis a surprise Crad Conover will be getting this noon — a meal early instead of late. I'll be too busy to bother with him when high noon comes, I'm thinking."

He was gone again, leaving Larkin alone with his thoughts once more. But now there was this to keep Larkin from the remembrance of a duty neglected, and the fetters made from a woman's charm: there was the beginning of a gnawing worry that centred around Banjo Sorenson, whose zeal should have made for promptness at the post of duty. It came to Larkin that he might take a turn about the town in search of his deputy; he had a need to be up and doing anyway, but still he sat, staring listlessly and trying not to think, and he was this way when he found a man in the doorway.

"Marshal?" the man asked.

He was a little fellow, colourless and nondescript, and there were a hundred like him, and Larkin had to take a long look before he remembered that he'd seen this one before. This man's name was Davis, and he'd been in Judge Bragg's court the night Banjo Sorenson had stood on trial for disturbing the peace of Santone Street. The man had been there with his wife, for he was the father of Jimmy Davis, who'd died in the dust before the Fandango. And Larkin said now, "What's on your mind, Davis?"

"The thousand dollars."

Larkin frowned, not understanding, and Davis said, "You were there that night and heard what was said. Judge Bragg fined Nick Diamond a thousand dollars and court costs. The thousand was to go to me and my missus on account of us losing Jimmy. Diamond said he'd send over the money the next morning, but he didn't. At least Judge Bragg never came around with it. And I can't find Bragg nowheres."

"I remember now," Larkin said.

"You've given Diamond until noon to clear out," Davis went on. "Everybody knows that. The way it adds up, Diamond will leave at noon, or he'll be killed. Either way, we'll never get the thousand dollars."

Larkin came to a stand. "There's time to

220

spare," he said. "I'll collect your money for you."

This, then, was his stimulus to action, this unforeseen event, this small and forgotten cog that turned a bigger wheel. He came out of the building and to the street; the sun was high enough to make itself felt, but all that met Larkin's eye promised nothing but peace. A few men lounged beneath the wooden awnings of various establishments, talking low and being very intent about their business; a dog sunned himself in the dust, and there was not a woman or a child to be seen. Swayback's main street was open for business, but it was a grim business that occupied it to-day.

Coming past the Chinaman's, Larkin saw Matt Hobbs inside, having a cup of coffee while waiting for the tray that would be taken over to Crad Conover. He lifted his hand to Hobbs and let it fall again, and then he turned off from this street, cutting between two buildings and coming to the water tank where he'd been attacked by Diamond's men on a night that seemed all of an eternity ago.

He paused here involuntarily, remembering how he'd pledged himself to stay aloof from the little quarrels of little men. He felt that old tingle of anticipation again, but he knew it now for what it was, the clamouring of nerves held taut by compulsion, the cry of a body that longed for peace. He looked at the sun and saw that it stood very high; it was after eleven, he judged, and found balm in the thought that the sunset would see the end to all this, another page turned and put behind him.

He began walking again; he came into Santone Street and found it locked in the same quiet lethargy that held the north end of town. Anticipation was here, too, but of a different kind. Beneath tugged-down hat-brims men gave him blank, unfathomable stares as he came along the boardwalk, and he strode along with his eyes ahead, and then he was at the Fandango and inside it, blinking in the lesser light. The bar had few patrons this morning, the gaming tables were nearly deserted, the piano silent and the curtains of the tiny stage were drawn shut. Nick Diamond was here, garbed in black broadcloth as always, but there was this one difference to-day: Diamond wore a gun-belt and a holstered forty-five, the weapon looking gigantic against his slight frame.

Diamond, sighting him, smiled, but there was no heart in it, and he drew a watch from his waistcoat pocket and had a look at it. He said, "You're thirty-five minutes early, Larkin. Or did you drop in for a drink?"

The scattering of customers didn't concern

Larkin; he knew their breed; they resented a badge's authority, but they always sat by and watched for the winner. If the Fandango were open at sundown, they'd cheer Diamond and call his victory their own. Meanwhile they'd merely wait, taking no sides. Larkin was doing his looking for Kinsella: there were others of Diamond's gun-hung gentry here, but Kinsella was the one he didn't want behind his back. The man was gone, and Larkin faced the bar and propped his elbows upon it; in this manner he could keep an eye on Diamond and on the man who worked behind the bar, and the long mirror gave him a command of any movement that was made in the room. He said, "There's a piece of unfinished business before the showdown, Nick. That thousand dollars for the Davises."

"The Davises?" Diamond said, and his bewilderment was as great as Larkin's had been.

"The parents of Jimmy Davis. You promised Bragg you'd give them a thousand dollars after that gun ruckus that killed the kid."

Diamond nodded. "I'd forgotten. I was to send it over the next morning. But I had my own misery to think about afterwards. You remember the window in Bragg's courtroom?"

"I remember," Larkin said. "Trot out the thousand, Nick."

"Of course. Did you think I wouldn't keep my word?"

"Sure, you'd keep it," Larkin said and wondered why anger rose in him when he faced this man. "You keep one side of your honour spotless so you can take it out and look at it whenever the stink of yourself gets too strong in your own nose. You're like the kind of deacon who prays on Sunday and forecloses a mortgage on Monday. You'll pay the thousand and preen yourself for doing it, and tomorrow you'd send your gunnies out to blast the street and kill another kid, if he happened to be in the way. Swayback will be well rid of you, Nick."

Diamond's laughter was harsh. "You're not going to be such a tough nut to crack, come high noon, Larkin. You're a talking man, and they make poor gunfighters."

"That," said Larkin, "is why I'm doing the talking *now*. Trot out the thousand, Nick."

"I don't carry that much in my till. Wait till I run up to my office, and I'll get it for you."

Larkin said, "I'll come along."

For a moment Diamond appraised him, his glance narrowing, and then he lifted his shoulders in a careless shrug and smiled his bewitching smile. "So you even doubt the spotless side of my honour," he said. "No,

Larkin, I wasn't going to bushwhack you from the top of the stairs. I want the town watching when I cut you down. Come along."

They went up the stairs elbow to elbow, and Diamond let them into his office. Larkin stood to one side of the door while Diamond delved into a desk drawer, and when a sheaf of currency was passed to him, Larkin counted it quickly and said, "That's right, Nick. An even thousand. Judge Bragg wasn't in his office this morning, but if you'll give me a piece of paper, I'll write a receipt in his name."

Diamond smiled again, but whatever he meant to say went unsaid, for Larkin suddenly lifted his head, his eyes questing the corners, and he said, *"What's that?"*

It was a sound so low as to be nothing more than the ghost of a sound. It was a dim thumping that had attracted Larkin's attention, and it might have been caused by anything. A person bound hand and foot and stretched upon a floor could have made such a sound by lifting his feet and dropping them.

Larkin said, "It's in the next room!" and he was mindful then that both Banjo Sorenson and Judge Bragg had apparently disappeared. He saw the quick movement that Diamond made, but his own hand was nearer a holster, and he said, "Easy, Nick! You wouldn't stand a show!"

Diamond placed his hands flat on the desk before him, and Larkin got to him and plucked Diamond's gun away and dropped it behind the desk. He said, "It's coming from the next room, Nick. How do I get in there?"

Diamond's lips peeled back from his teeth, and he said, "I'd have let you walk out of here, Larkin. I'd have waited till high noon. Don't make it hard for yourself, mister."

"The next room," Larkin said. "Take me there."

This might have been their moment, their showdown, but Diamond stood disarmed now, and that gave him no choice. A man could read death in another's eyes, and it was in Larkin's. With a shrug of surrender, Diamond came around the desk and opened the door and stepped a few paces to the next door and, fishing a key from his pocket, unlocked and opened that door. This was Melody's room, and Melody was here, and so was Banjo Sorenson, the two of them bound and gagged and stretched upon the floor.

Larkin said, "Get those ropes off them, Nick."

Diamond hesitated, his eyes black with hatred, and still Larkin didn't draw a gun. But Diamond knelt and fell to work, and when Banjo Sorenson stood free, the giant rubbed at his wrists, saying nothing, his eyes blank and his yellow mane tousled, and then he brushed past Larkin in that same mesmerised silence and went pounding down the stairs. When the gag was taken from Melody's mouth, she said, "He's gone after Kinsella, Mr. Larkin. Kinsella's the man who owned those spurs Banjo had."

Larkin steadied her as she came to her feet, but he never let her get between himself and Diamond. He said, "Did they hurt you?" The question was almost casual, but Nick Diamond's life waited on the answer.

She said, "They tied us up last night and left us locked in here. I can guess that Diamond had the key, and not Kinsella. No, I've suffered no harm. Can we get out of here?"

"I reckon," Larkin said.

"King Conover's raiding the town at high noon to-day! Isn't it almost noon, now? Kinsella told me about it when he thought he had me trapped here."

Larkin said, "You don't need to look at her that way, Nick. I'd already guessed that Conover was coming." Putting his hand behind him, he fumbled for the key Diamond had left in the opened door. "I'm locking this door as we go out, Nick. I wouldn't start hammering on it right away. The panelling is too thin to stop a bullet."

Drawing Melody with him, he backed from

the room. He pulled the door shut and twisted the key, then took it from the keyhole and hurled it away. Then he went down the stairs with Melody, his left arm around her waist, supporting her, his right arm swinging free. The bartender saw them first, his startled glance betraying his surprise, and Larkin lifted his voice. "Put those fat paws of yours in sight on top of the bar," he ordered. "There, that's right. Now keep them there."

Melody said, "The place has a back door."

But he brought her through the bar-room, and no man made a move. When they were beyond the bartender, Larkin swung out, backing towards the batwings, and he shoved them outwards with his spine and went through them, and still the silence held. Then they were outside and hurrying up the boardwalk, and Melody was pouring a babble of talk into his ear.

"I'd been listening to them through the wall of my room," she said. "They found that out, somehow, and they made wild talk of a dawn raid of Conover's last night, and then Kinsella followed me to Judge Bragg's. Bragg promised to get word to you, or to head into the hills by himself to stop Conover."

"Bragg did?" Larkin said in great surprise and saw the shape of an astounding truth.

"When I came back, I met Banjo. He was

228

going to force me to tell him which one of the Fandango men owned the broken spur he carried. He's told you about that spur, I suppose. It was Kinsella he wanted, but I knew Kinsella would kill him. I persuaded him to wait while I went after my things. We were going to be married. But Kinsella cornered me, and Banjo came, and Nick caught the both of us."

He said soothingly, "There . . . there. . . . It's all over now. I'll have you beyond the tracks in a few minutes."

Then they heard the shot; it was dim with distance, but it broke the heavy hush that held this town, and Larkin knew instantly that the gun had been fired to the north, over yonder on Swayback's main street. There was just that one shot, and then the silence closed down again, only to be broken by three closely spaced shots that were like a tocsin; and after that many guns blared. Larkin glanced skyward. It was nearly noon, and only then did he realise how much time he had spent on Santone Street. King Conover had come, and the trap was being sprung.

CHAPTER XIV

Down from the hills in the early dawn light King Conover had come riding, a man big and blocky in the saddle, and behind him trailed the full strength of his crew, ten in all. They came silently, threading the familiar timbered trails in single file, and bunching up on the flat, sage-speckled land that spread below the Silver Belts. They came sullenly; they had toiled through the night to restore the damage done to their bridge by the blade of Joshua Bragg, and they'd gotten the severed ropes spliced and strong enough to hold a man's weight, but this had cost them their sleep. They'd worked under the sharp goad of Conover's tongue, pitting themselves against the marching hours; but now they were on their way. And with them rode Judge Joshua Bragg. He was along by King Conover's wish, was Bragg. He sat an unsteady saddle, barely conscious but able to cling to the horn, the white of a makeshift bandage showing beneath his black, broad-brimmed hat. He came with vacant, uncomprehending eyes, a man heedless of his whereabouts and pain-racked to a point beyond caring. Or so it seemed to those who kept a careful watch over him. There had been dissension when Conover had proposed bringing Bragg along, but the King had roared it down.

"We've got to fetch a spare saddler into Swayback," Conover had observed. "Crad will need a cayuse after I've sprung him out of the calaboose. An empty saddle catches the eye quicker than a full one, and as long as we've found this jigger's horse, we might as well put it to use. I tell you that having the judge along will be our protection on the way in!"

"By God!" said the one whose gun had laid Bragg low. "Haven't you had enough of his snakiness, King? He'll tangle our twine as quick as we hit town!"

"He had no key to Crad's cell," Conover rumbled. "That was pure bluff, I reckon. But when I ride into Swayback, he rides beside me. And when I march into that jail, he marches in ahead — with a gun at his spine. If he knows any tricks for getting a cell open fast, he'll use them then."

"I'd be a heap happier if he was beefed and dumped into the gorge," the dissenter argued.

"He'll be dead — when I've finished with him," King Conover promised. "I'll leave him dead in Crad's cell, so that any other man who ever thinks of running a sandy on King Conover will have the sight of him to remember.

Meanwhile, though, he comes along if he's able to sit a saddle."

And so it had been decided, for he was still the law among them. Besides, he was in no mood for the opinions of others this morning, for a worry was gnawing at him, and he was irritable and morose. One of his men had gone into Swayback last night on special business for him; that man had not returned. There was the smell of trouble in such failure, but there could be no changing the plans now, not at this late hour. Conover's one consolation was that the man he'd dispatched had been close-mouthed and picked with care for the mission. The law would get no truth out of that one if they had him in their toils.

And now King Conover's crew came riding across the dew-spangled rangeland, and Swayback lay ahead, misty in the first sunlight. All the long waiting and planning was ended. All the nerve-fraying days of inactivity were behind them. They came keyed for the job ahead, eager with the promise of excitement, stolidly drunk on the heady brew of anticipation. When they talked, it was of how they would spend their loot, but mostly they held to a tight-lipped silence, for they were like race-horses coming to the post, taut and straining.

Such were the men that Judge Bragg found

around him as his head gradually cleared, but he gave no sign that his faculties were returning. He had tasted despair last night at the bridge; he tasted it again now, for though he'd heard no part of King Conover's plan, he could guess what his own end would be. He had won a measure of Conover's respect; he could see it in the outlaw's studied glance, for a man who'd ridden with Quantrell could admire the nerve Bragg had shown last night. But it was the respect of the firing-squad leader for the man who refuses the blindfold. It was the respect of the hangman who adjusts the noose about the neck of one who has walked unfalteringly to the gallows. It brought Bragg no peace of mind.

Looking down at his hands, Bragg saw that they were trembling, and he clutched more tightly at the saddle-horn. They'd left him unbound, but he was weaponless and surrounded, and fettered by these very facts. Off to the south, he saw the lazy lift of smoke from the Boxed-C ranch-house, and he remembered the crew of Cultus Pierce and longed for the sight of those lean, wind-burned riders, but Conover was giving the spread a wide berth.

The miles fell behind them, the town drew nearer as the sun arched upwards in its slow climb to zenith, and it was perhaps eleven o'clock when Conover halted his cavalcade, dismounted and climbed to a low bluff and had a look at Swayback through a pair of field-glasses. He was a long time at this reconnoitering; the sun grew hot against the nape of Bragg's neck; but at last the field-glasses were restored to Conover's saddle-bag, and the outlaw swung up to his saddle. "Looks good," he told his men. "Not many people on the street as near as I could make out. We'll split up now."

They waited, sitting slaunchwise in their saddles, all of them with their eyes upon him, for this was his way, to assign them to their posts only at the last minute. He knew their courage, did Conover, and he knew their individual capabilities, and he knew also that a man with his job cut out for him far in advance lived his work over and over again in his mind in the last few hours, and that made for nervousness. So he gave them nothing to dwell upon until the time was at hand.

Now he said, "We'll drift into town in twos and threes. Old goat-whiskers, here, will be with me, and we'll head straight for the jail. The Wind River Kid, Joe and Grant will take care of the horses; we'll bunch some of the cayuses before the bank, the rest at hitch-rails close by. But not so near that anybody will get suspicious. One of you boys will stay with each bunch of horses. Stick close to them, but not too close."

Three men nodded.

"Yakima, you'll go inside and cover the cashier," Conover went on. "Pete and Laramie and Ben, you ride into town with Yakima, and go into the bank with him. Pete and Ben will cover any customers who happen to be in the bank at the time. Laramie, you load the stuff into the tow-sack. Don't burden yourself down too much with silver, but get every greenback in the place. If there's only a few people inside, Pete can give you a hand with the stuff while Ben keeps a drop on the folks."

Conover looked at the man who'd ridden with him the longest, and his association with this one went back to Kansas days and Quantrell. "Baldy, you stay in your saddle and wait up the street. You know where. Laramie will fetch you a full tow-sack as quick as it's loaded. Kirby, you and Buck will hang around just outside the bank and let Yakima and the boys know if anybody comes along, or if anything looks wrong. And I don't want any of you boys with the horses to get jumpy and start doing Kirby and Buck's work. Now have you all got everything straight?"

When they nodded, Conover glanced again towards Swayback, and the worry was re-born in his eyes. "I'd like to know why Mojave never showed back last night."

One said, "He's either dead or in jail. If he's dead, he's dead, and we'll spend his split. If he's in jail, you'll find him when you go after Crad."

Conover said, "If we time this right, I'll be coming out of the jail with Crad just about the same moment you boys will be hitting saddles with the tow-sack full. Laramie, you take the sack to Baldy. Then we turn south to Santone Street. All of us, except Baldy. We're going to tree that town like it never was treed before."

Some nudged their horses, but Conover held up his hand for their attention. "One more thing," he said. "Matt Hobbs. He's my personal meat, do you savvy? I'm leaving him dead for the job he did of outsmarting me the night I was to meet him at Pierce's line shack."

That was what put the new fear in Joshua Bragg, and the courage, too. He sat in a stupefied silence, pretending not to listen while Conover had issued orders, deploying his men, but he had heard everything, and he saw now the smooth efficiency with which this job was to be handled. He could even admire the careful generalship of King Conover; he liked a man with his wits about him, but he hadn't thought of Matt Hobbs in connection with all this. He risked a look at the sun and saw that it was drawing close to zenith, and he drew some scant consolation from that. Perhaps Matt Hobbs would be down on Santone Street with Dave Larkin. But this crew was heading for Santone Street once their work to the north of the tracks was finished. Bragg sighed a long and impotent sigh and found Conover beside him.

"You're riding in with me," Conover said. "You'll behave natural when we hit the street. Do you savvy that? You'll behave natural, because the first foolish move you make will be the death of you."

Then Bragg was riding stirrup to stirrup with Conover as the group split into small knots, each moving upon the town from a different angle. Conover kept his horse at a walk, and Bragg did likewise, and thus he saw others enter the town before them, and when they rode into the outskirts, the one called Baldy was already stationed beneath the giant cottonwood across from Sheldon Abbott's house, the man giving no sign of recognition as Conover and Bragg rode past him.

The main street seemed singularly deserted when they rode into it; a few men lounged beneath wooden awnings, and some of these lifted their hands to Bragg in salute, and he returned these waves stiffly, praying in his heart that at least one among the loungers would know King Conover for whom he was. Conover slouched indolently in his saddle, but he had his sombrero brim pulled low. The outlaw said, "Grin, damn you! Grin and pretend you've no worry on your mind. If one of those men so much as looks at you like he thinks something's wrong, it will be the same as if *you* made a mistake!"

They came past the livery stable and the mercantile store, and beyond this was a weed-grown lot, and then the frame bank building. Farther on was the high lift of the town hall, and, across from it, the jail building. The Wind River Kid stood among four horses that were tied at the bank's hitch-rail. Two other outlaws were with horses at nearby hitch-rails, and two men lounged before the bank. The other four had gone inside the building, Bragg judged.

Conover swung past the bank, looking neither to the right nor the left, and in these taut moments Bragg had to admire the man's remarkable coolness. Racking his horse before the town hall, Conover stepped down from his saddle and gestured to Bragg to do likewise. Conover said then, "You're walking ahead of me across the street and into the jail."

The ground felt unsteady to Bragg; his head

reeled, and he was glad the bullet that had creased his scalp had bitten no deeper. He was without a plan at this moment; he could do nothing but obey, and he faced towards the jail and so did Conover, and horror rushed through Bragg then and threatened to unhinge his knees. A man was in the doorway of the jail building at that very moment, a man who wore a chalky, colourless slicker that was all too familiar, and this man was bearing a tray and stepping along carefully and slowly. The doorway was shadowy, but Bragg saw him — and King Conover saw him, too.

Everything that happened then happened quickly. Conover cursed and said, *"Hobbs!"* and Conover dragged out his gun, but for Joshua Bragg there was no weapon but his wits. Blindly he bent and scooped up a handful of the dust of the street and hurled it into the eyes of King Conover. Conover's gun roared, and for a fleeting, fearful moment Bragg thought that the outlaw had fired at him, and his fear was even greater when he realised that he stood unscathed. For the man in the doorway was swung around by the shock of King Conover's bullet; he flung up his slicker-clad arms and the tray went clattering, and the man, falling backwards down the steps and to the boardwalk, fell to his death. . . .

Most of this morning Crad Conover had been at the barred window of his cell; from here he had an oblique glimpse of the main street, and, long before the sun reached zenith, he had guessed that something significant portended in Swayback to-day. That this was the day Dave Larkin was driving Nick Diamond from town, he knew. Matt Hobbs had told him so when the ex-marshal had fetched the supper tray last evening. That King Conover was raiding the town to-day to free him from jail, he didn't know. But he suspected the truth.

He was brother to the King; he had learned wiliness from King Conover, and all the strategy of the owlhoot; he had patterned himself after the King; he had geared his brain to think as King Conover thought, and he knew more of the workings of the King's mind than did any other man. Also he knew of the alliance between Santone Street and the high hills, for Nick Diamond and King Conover had formed their secret partnership before Crad's capture. To-day Nick Diamond would be needing help, and to-day King Conover would likely come to his aid.

This, then, might be Crad's last day of imprisonment, and it was for the sight of King Conover that he watched the street. His vigil gave him a glimpse of many men, but not of his brother; Matt Hobbs was busying himself upon the street, passing through Crad's range of vision many times.

And then Crad saw men with rifles gathering to talk low-voiced and these same men dispersing later, and after that the street became strangely silent and deserted.

All this Crad saw, and there were many ways such signs could be interpreted. The town was arming to back Dave Larkin in his march against Santone Street. The town was arming to stand ready if needed. Or — and this was the thought that turned him desperate — the town, too, had guessed that King Conover might be coming today, and the men of Swayback were ready and waiting.

But how could they know? Who could have guessed that King Conover would have an interest in the affairs of Nick Diamond? Not Matt Hobbs. Dave Larkin, then? But all of this was guesswork, and Crad wondered if he were borrowing worry, but the fear persisted and his desperation with it.

If King Conover came, the sign said that the King would ride into a trap. And so thinking, Crad Conover remembered his carefully nurtured plans for escape and realised then that a greater need than his own must see him out of here, and quickly. At the window again, he saw Matt Hobbs go into the Chinaman's, and not long after that Dave Larkin crossed his range of vision and was gone, and, after an interminable wait, Hobbs came from the restaurant bearing a tray.

It was not quite noon, and Hobbs had never been prompt with the meals, yet Hobbs was coming now, and that fact seemed suddenly very significant to Crad Conover. There was something in the wind for sure — something that was upsetting Hobbs' careless routine, and the desperation rose in Crad Conover until it was beyond denying, and he knew that he must make his play at once. A washstand stood here in his cell — a stand with a basin, a pitcher of water, a bar of soap and a coarse towel. Quickly he worked the soap into a lather; he heard the front door creak open as Hobbs entered with the tray, and Crad broke off a corner of the soap bar and thrust it into his mouth.

When Hobbs came through the ante-room and down the cell corridor to pause before the door, Crad Conover was down upon the floor, writhing and clutching his stomach and beating his heels against the planking in pretended agony, and there was a froth upon his lips. Hobbs peered hard and said, "What in thunder's ailing ye?" But Crad Conover made him no coherent answer.

Hobbs laid the tray upon the corridor floor and fumbled with his keys and got the door open and came into the cell. This was an ancient dodge, this pretending to be sick to fetch a jailer inside, but the froth on Conover's lips was the added realistic touch that disarmed Hobbs, just as Conover had judged it would. Hobbs bent over him anxiously, and Crad Conover's slim brown fingers came up and closed upon Hobbs' scrawny throat, cutting off any outcry, and the two of them went rolling the width of the cell, fighting frantically.

The wiry strength of Crad Conover made the telling difference; youth was on his side, and when he brought his fists up into Hobbs' face again and again, the old man went limp beneath him, and Conover arose, panting and dishevelled, to gaze upon the stunned and bleeding Hobbs. Crad's first act was to snatch away Hobbs' forty-five and tuck it into the waistband of his trousers. Then, mindful that he'd have to get out of this building undetected, he picked up Hobbs' shapeless sombrero and placed it on his head and tugged the brim low.

Cat-footing out into the corridor, he came into the little ante-room to the front of the building and peered from its small, dirty window. Here he could see a section of the street; there were only a few people about, but there were a number of horses at the hitch-rail before the bank, and most of them looked speedy. Also, there was a man among them, and that gave Crad some concern. The man had his back to Crad and was lazily fashioning a cigarette, it seemed, and thus he didn't recognise the Wind River Kid.

The next five minutes would count — the next five minutes and the fifty feet or so that lay between the door of this building and the closest hitch-rack that could serve him. Casting his eyes about the room, Crad spied the long colourless slicker of Matt Hobbs' that hung from a wall peg, and he donned the garment. He was a taller man than Hobbs, and most people would recognise that fact in a minute, so he stooped his shoulders. Then he remembered the thing that would make the one perfect touch to his disguise, and he went back into the corridor and picked up the tray Hobbs had placed on the floor before entering the cell. Hobbs was stirring restlessly and lifting one arm weakly. Crad Conover returned quickly to the front of the building with the tray, and he fumbled with the door leading to the street and got it open.

He must move slowly now, he knew, for, once beyond this doorway, he'd come into the stark sunshine of the noon hour. He remembered Hobbs' limp and emulated it as he took a step forward, and all the while he kept his eyes downwards as a man will do who is burdened and has to step carefully. This was another advantage of toting the tray; it would appear natural to any onlooker that his head should be bent, and it would keep that same onlooker from catching a real glimpse of his face.

Someone cried *"Hobbs!"* That voice was King Conover's! Crad Conover lifted his eyes in amazement, and he saw King Conover dragging at his gun, and he saw Joshua Bragg scoop up a handful of dust and hurl it into King Conover's eyes at the same time. And in that same split-second the gun roared.

The bullet struck Crad full in the chest, and he let go of the tray as he swung around by the impact. He felt himself falling, and he tried hard to get a hold on something; he took a lurching, backward step and that put him through the doorway, and he tumbled down towards the boardwalk and struck it, and went rolling into the dust of the street. He cried, *"King! . . . King!"* And then the life went out of him. . . .

This was the sight Judge Bragg saw, but only Crad's agonised voice could have brought the truth to King Conover, for the dust was still in the outlaw's eyes. Conover took a blind, tottering step forward, and another, the gun slipped from his hand and went down into the dust unheeded, and then he was lurching to Crad and kneeling beside him and gathering Crad up into his arms and calling to him hoarsely. He was alone at that instant, alone with his dead, a crouching, gibbering hulk of a man.

The Wind River Kid, yonder with the horses at the bank's hitch-rail, had been electrified by the shot, and so had the two who loitered before the bank's open doorway, but all of them stood indecisively. Here was the strength and the weakness of King Conover's kind of discipline; not one of the three deserted his post, but none was prepared for such an emergency as this one. Seeing this, Joshua Bragg picked up Conover's fallen gun and came softly towards the big outlaw and tapped him on the shoulder.

"You're under arrest, suh," Bragg said, but he wasn't sure that Conover heard him. A look of madness was in Conover's eyes, and it would still be there when he stood trial in the weeks to come, and when he climbed the gallows to taste the rope law Montana meted out to rustlers.

Suddenly, Matt Hobbs was in the jail-building's doorway, his hand raised falteringly to his forehead, and he had one look at the tableau the street presented, and then he came limping swiftly down the steps and took the gun from Bragg and lifted it to the sky and fired three times.

That brought the street to life, the thunder of hidden guns became a trump of judgment, but still King Conover crouched in the dust with a dead man in his arms, and the look of the lost in his eyes.

Sig Kinsella came into a bar-room that was big with emptiness; gunfire's blatant tocsin to the north of the tracks had drawn the morning's skimpy patronage outside, and half-finished drinks and strewn playing-cards upon the tables evidenced hasty departures. But Nick Diamond was here. Hope had fled from Diamond, and with it had gone surety, leaving only desperation and a hate born of frustration. This Kinsella saw at once, and his own hands lost their steadiness.

Kinsella said, "Do you know what's going on up there?" And he tipped his head to the north.

"I can guess," Diamond said. "One by one my boys have gone out for a look. None of them have come back. None of them will. The rats leave the sinking ship." He appraised Kinsella with a flash of his old scorn. "What's keeping you from a fast saddle?"

Kinsella said, "You made me your right arm. When they think of you, they'll think of me. That ties us together, whether we like it or not. And we've got only one card left to play — those two upstairs. Have you let Larkin know that we're holding them?"

"Larkin was here not long ago," Diamond said. "He followed me to my office, and he heard the girl making a noise in the next room. He got me under a gun. We've no hole-card now."

The blood left Kinsella's face. "That Swede's loose and looking for me."

"Sorenson went out of here like he was shot from a gun, Sig. Or so the apron told me after he got me out of Melody's room, where Larkin left me locked."

Kinsella looked from door to door, and his fear was so manifest that Diamond found a strange, macabre delight in it. Kinsella said, "Sorenson will follow me wherever we go. A helluva mess this turned out to be!"

Diamond remembered that his destiny was tied irrevocably to this lean and wiry man's, and the delight went out of him. He said, "And Larkin will follow me. He thinks he'll be satisfied to drive me out, but if I run, he'll take my trail. He can't help it. He hates me, and I hate him, and we both knew it the first day we sized each other up. There's only one finish between us."

The distant gunfire was diminishing; whatever was happening north of the tracks was nearly over now. Kinsella said, "He'll be down here before many minutes. Do you mean that you're going to meet him?"

Diamond nodded. "Gun against gun. That will keep the rest of the town out of it. We'll face each other out there on the street."

"You're sharp with a six-shooter," Kinsella conceded. "I wonder if you're that sharp."

Diamond's face darkened, and his hate stood naked in his eyes. "Go across the street to the Amarillo House," he ordered. "Climb to the second storey hallway, and you'll find a ladder leading up to a trapdoor set in the roof. When you're on to the roof and faced towards the street, you'll find that the false front shuts off most of your view, but there's a hole in that false front big enough to let a rifle barrel through and to give you a good glimpse of what's going on below. I know. I climbed up there and had a look around a long time ago. Before I found that Matt Hobbs wasn't likely to be any real worry to me."

Kinsella drew in his breath. "Then what?" he demanded. "I can cut Larkin down from the roof. Likely Sorenson won't be far away from Larkin, and probably I'll be able to get the Swede, too. But the town will tear us apart just the same."

Diamond said, "I've thought this thing through, Sig. It's our one chance. While you're getting on top of the Amarillo, I'll find the two fastest horses on Santone Street and tie them out behind this building. When Larkin shows up, I'll speak my piece, and he'll agree to it. Man to man. If there's a crowd at his back, the crowd will scatter for cover and let us make our play. When I start walking towards him, we'll have a stretch of the street to ourselves."

"And that's when I pick him off?"

Diamond nodded. "When he drops, it will take most of those fools a few minutes to guess that it wasn't my gun that dropped him. And we'll be using those minutes. I'll wheel back into here and cut through the building and pile into a saddle. I'll lead the other horse around to the back of the Amarillo House. You come down that covered stairway to the alley and join me. We'll be showing all of them our heels out of Swayback before they wake up."

Kinsella said thoughtfully, "It means that Larkin drives us out, but we leave him dead. I'll like that." He went behind the bar, plumbed under the long counter and found a rifle and inspected it. But, with the rifle crooked under his arm, he paused at the batwings, his eyes aflame with a sudden suspicion. "You wouldn't get excited, Nick, and forget to bring that spare horse around to the back of the Amarillo House?"

Diamond smiled. "This is the last chore you'll do for me in Swayback, Sig. It will leave me beholden to you for the rest of my life. No, we'll ride out together."

The batwings bobbed behind Kinsella, and Diamond gave him a minute to be gone and then walked to the rear door of the Fandango and stepped outside and into a lean-to that clung to the building. Here he kept his own horse, a leggy mount that had won him racing money in other parts. But there was only this one horse. As he carefully saddled the animal, Nick Diamond was remembering the ancient adage which decreed that the man who travelled the swiftest was the man who travelled alone. . . .

Larkin, racing out of Santone Street with Melody panting beside him, came to the water tank at the railroad tracks and paused. To the north, gunfire beat in ragged bursts, and now Larkin could hear the strident shouting of many men, the pounding of frantic hoofs, and he said, "You'd better wait here while I go on. Sounds like a lot of loose lead flying around up that way. Head for the town hall a little later. You'll be safe there."

She said, "Be careful."

But already he was sprinting away, and when he came between two buildings and on to the main street, he saw chaos. The bank had emptied, and some of Conover's men had gotten into saddles and some hadn't, for the three shots Matt Hobbs had fired — the shots Larkin had heard over on Santone Street a few minutes before — had unleashed the hidden guns of Swayback. From the slots between buildings, and from the doorways of mercantile store and saloon and livery stable, the guns were blaring, and men were down writhing in the dust of the street, dust that had been churned by many hoofs, and the smell of it was in the air, and the heavy acrid odour of powder-smoke was everywhere.

A cayuse thundered towards Larkin on a dead run, the rider bent low in the saddle, and Larkin got a glimpse of the man's frenzied face and remembered him from the ledge in the high hills. With the sunlight flashing on the man's gun, Larkin brought one of his own out of leather and fired first. The man was lifted out of his saddle, but Larkin was never to be sure that his bullet had done that, for a dozen guns had spoken simultaneously. The panicked cayuse bolted onwards; and Larkin, sweeping the street with a long glance, saw no other target, but he kept his gun in his hand.

Spying Judge Bragg carefully emerging from the jail building, Larkin ran to him and said, "So you're back! Where's Hobbs?"

"Yonder, suh," Bragg said with solemn dignity, the wave of his arm indicating the far end of the street. "He's directing the operations of our valiant citizenry. I, suh, have just locked King Conover in the cell his brother occupied. Arrested him singlehanded, suh."

There was much here that Larkin didn't understand, for Hobbs and Bragg had carried Crad Conover's body into the town hall before Hobbs had gone to take command of Swayback's men, but Bragg quickly supplied the missing pieces. Far away, off towards the town's outskirts, the guns still spoke, but this street had turned quiet again. Larkin said, "It's all worked out better than I'd planned. You're a good man, Judge. And, from the sound of things, I'd say that the boys have everything just about in order at this end of town. Will you find Hobbs for me and tell him I've headed back to Santone Street? It's a little past high noon, now."

Bragg said politely, "If I can be of any other assistance, suh — ?"

Larkin said, "You can, Judge. If I don't come back this way, there'll be a girl from Santone Street who'll be coming to the town hall. I owe her a great deal. Will you see that all of Swayback remembers that?"

Bragg nodded. "Yes," he said.

Larkin turned then, had his look at the

townsmen who were swarming the street, and went his solitary way between two buildings and back towards Santone Street. He walked slowly; he knew that now his moment was coming, his solitary moment when he would stand alone as he'd always stood alone, and he neither anticipated nor deplored the thing that had to be done. He had ceased to be a personality; he had turned himself into the steel of the guns that rode at his thighs; he was without soul and without thought, and it had always been thus in these last, bleak minutes. Yet he'd thought that this was for ever behind him, and there was room for one small regret. He was remembering the bit of land he'd meant to buy, the house he'd intended to build. He'd lost that dream in Swayback; no matter what awaited him on Santone Street, he'd lost that for ever.

He came back to reality at the sound of his name, and he turned to find a dozen men following after him. They were some of Swayback's citizenry, and they were armed and formidable of appearance, and Larkin guessed that Hobbs had witnessed his departure and sent these men to back him. The one in the lead said, "Hobbs will be busy locking up what's left of Conover's crew. The rest are dead. Maybe you'll need us on Santone Street — maybe not. One of our boys saw Diamond's crew cutting out of town shortly after we sprung the trap on Conover's men."

Larkin said, "Come along, if you wish."

And so he came to Santone Street with these men at his back, and there was this consolation in their presence: he could leave Swayback when his work was done, and leave with the assurance that no other Nick Diamond would arise to supplant the one he'd kill or exile this day. These men would see to that. They had needed arousing, and they'd been aroused; and the pride of having defended their town was strong in them. They would keep that pride, and it would give them vigilance. Swayback had shaped its own destiny this day.

And yet there was still this one last thing that had to be done; there was that one man who was already defeated and deserted but who would not accept defeat because of his own puny code; and it was always this way. And so he came down the silent, empty board-walk of the street, and when he was within a hundred yards of the Fandango the bat-wings parted and Nick Diamond stepped into view. Cupping his hands to his mouth, Di-amond cried, "Larkin! There's only me. Do you need all those men at your back?" Larkin said, "That depends on you, Nick. Are you taking that train out?" And all the while he was walking forward.

Diamond said, "You're talking like a badge-toter, but you're thinking differently. You're hoping I'll try to stay. We both know that. Let's have it out between us."

Larkin spoke over his shoulder to the men following him. "You heard him," he said.

That scattered them to the right and to the left; they went scurrying to whatever scanty cover they could find, and Larkin paced on forward, narrowing the distance between himself and Diamond to half, and he said then, "Start your play whenever you're ready, Nick."

Diamond stripped off his black coat and let it drop to the porch of the Fandango, and Larkin understood that move; Diamond wanted nothing in his way when he reached for the gun at his thigh. Diamond came down into the dust of the street then; there were only the two of them here in the strong sunlight, two with a stretch of empty distance between them; and the silence hung over Swayback once again.

Now all of this was becoming a familiar ritual; Larkin tugged hard at the brim of his hat, wanting no sun in his eyes, and after that he let his hands dangle limply, for the next gesture he would make would signal action. He came forward at a slow, relentless pace; he saw that Diamond was adopting that same measured stride; the distance grew less, and it came to Larkin that his hate lessened with it and then was gone, and Diamond was no more to him than a cardboard target against a wall. Yet all this time Larkin kept his eyes on Diamond's right hand, knowing that when that hand moved, the play would be made.

To him, then, the world had narrowed down to this one man, and he watched Diamond and shut off his mind and his senses to all else, and thus he had no warning of treachery, no instinct to tell him that the real danger lay atop the roof of the Amarillo House, ahead and above him. But when the rifle roared, he knew the blare of it for what it was, and he sensed that the sound was high and distant, but at that same moment Diamond's hand fell towards the man's holster.

Larkin got his own gun out and fired, his action smooth and co-ordinated, but the roar of the rifle had disconcerted him for the merest fraction of a second, and Diamond's shot was first. Larkin felt the bullet tug at the brim of his hat, and he thought: *The fool! Why didn't he aim at my body?* Diamond's white waistcoat made a fine target; Larkin's gun bucked back against his hand, and he knew he had made his hit. Diamond turned around on one heel; Larkin saw the man toss his gun aside as though it had suddenly grown very hot and

258

very heavy, and when Diamond went down into the dust, Larkin knew that he was dead.

That rifle was speaking again, and Larkin had located the sound. Behind him men were pouring into the street and charging towards him, the men of Swayback who'd followed him here, and they were coming with questions and with congratulations, but he had no time to wait for them. He went sprinting towards the Amarillo House and into its stuffy lobby, and he found the ancient clerk behind his desk.

Larkin shouted, "How do I get to the roof?"

"Ladder . . . upstairs," the old fellow quavered, and Larkin mounted the steps and groped frantically in the dimness of the hall until he found the ladder. It led upwards to an open trapdoor, and he bobbed through this and to the roof. There'd be two men here, he knew; that rifle had been fired from this roof, *but not at him*. He could grasp Diamond's treachery now; Kinsella was here, and Kinsella had been posted thus for only one reason. But Kinsella had not had his chance to fire into the street, for Banjo Sorenson had found him here, and Banjo was closing in upon Kinsella. Diamond's man stood with his back to the false front, the rifle at his hip, and he fired wildly, blindly, not even seeing Larkin.

There was blood on Sorenson, and the

Swede was a man more dead than alive, but still he came lurching towards Kinsella, and the sight was magnificent enough to engrave itself for ever upon Larkin's memory. Kinsella screamed in terror and tossed the rifle aside and went running towards the trapdoor. He saw Larkin then, and he swerved aside, darting to the rear of the roof, but Banjo was hard after him, and Banjo closed with the man, and the two of them became locked together.

Larkin came running towards them, his intent to pull them apart, for he knew that Banjo, hard hit and bleeding, could be no match for Kinsella's desperate fury. But Larkin came too late. Entwined, the two men went reeling towards the edge of the roof, and there was no false front to block the way. Larkin saw the dying Banjo's intent, then, and he cried out hoarsely, his own voice unreal in his ears. With Kinsella forced backwards by Banjo, the two stumbled and went over the edge together and were lost from Larkin's sight.

Kinsella's long-drawn-out scream of fear and anguish was in Larkin's ears when he came to the edge of the roof and peered downwards. Sweeping his hand before his eyes, Larkin turned and lurched back towards the trapdoor. Nausea threatened to overcome him; he fought against this and descended to the hallway and found the rear stairs that he and Amy had once used. And he came down into the alley to find the two, their grip broken at last, lying there.

Both were alive, and Larkin went to Banjo first and saw blood on the big Scandinavian's lips. But Banjo smiled and said, "I see him creeping into the hotel, and I followed him, but I ban looking one damn' long time before I figure he's gone to roof." His voice faded, and Larkin thought this was the end of it. But Banjo said distinctly, "I fixed him! I fixed him *goot!*" And he smiled again and, smiling, died.

Kinsella was cursing in a low, monotonous voice, and Larkin bent over him then and listened, his lips tightening. Men came pouring around the building, but Kinsella was dead when they reached him, and there was a babble of questions and ejaculations, and suddenly Larkin found Matt Hobbs here.

Hobbs put his hand to Larkin's shoulder, and he said, "Diamond's dead, they tell me, and here's Kinsella dead, too. King Conover and what's left of his crew is in jail. 'Tis a good day's work, Dave."

"Anybody hurt in the bank?"

Hobbs shook his head. "Ye recollect that the boys wasn't to open up on Conover's crew till I gave them the signal? When I got my chance to start the shooting, Conover's bunch had already loaded a tow-sack with currency, and when they came rampagin' out of the bank, they fetched that tow-sack along. The one who was packing it got into a saddle, and some of the boys gave him chase. He was a wily one, that Conover. He had one of his men, a bald old jigger, posted out near the edge of town, and on the fastest horse. The man with the tow-sack reached the bald feller and gave him the sack. Do ye see the idea? If things went wrong, we were supposed to give chase to the wrong man."

"But it didn't work?"

Hobbs frowned. "The boys got both of 'em, but we didn't find the sack. Things were happening so lively that nobody's sure just how the trick was worked. But my idea is that Conover's men, seeing that the jig was up, tossed the sack away so they wouldn't be burdened with it. Likely it's in the weeds somewhere out there by the edge of town. Now that all the fuss is over, I'll put every man to hunting for it."

"There's no need, Matt," Larkin said. "I know where your money sack went to. I'll get it for you."

Astonishment made Hobbs ludicrous, but all he said was, "Do ye need any help?"

Larkin said, "I'll go alone." And he turned then and headed northwards towards the distant house of Sheldon Abbott.

Amy admitted him when Larkin mounted to the porch and knocked upon the door, and she looked very small and very frightened, and there were no words between them. She took him directly to the living-room where Abbott sat in his wheel-chair, and the man's long face clouded with a frown when he saw who had come. Abbott said, "It's about time someone showed up to tell me what's been going on! After all, I'm still the mayor of this town. Guns have been banging from one end of Swayback to another, and just a short while ago I saw a man shot out of his saddle almost at my very doorstep. Have all of you been too busy to report?"

His petulance was convincing enough; Larkin conceded that, and, studying the man, he could understand how Sheldon Abbott had kept all Swayback fooled. There were the King Conovers with their swift savagery, the men who used boldness as a club; there were the Nick Diamonds who were given to sly scheming and treachery, but you could read such men a mile away. Here was a more insidious kind of villainy. Here was something made of hypocrisy and a pretence too deep for ready detection, and here sat the greatest enemy Swayback had ever had.

Knowing this, Larkin said, "The story's short and simple, Abbott. King Conover and Nick Diamond were in cahoots. Conover came to-day to raid the bank and free his brother — and to help Diamond at the same time. I was expecting them, so I had Matt Hobbs set a trap, with the townsmen backing us. Conover walked into it. After we'd gotten his twine all tangled for him, I went to call on Diamond. We shot it out, and Diamond is dead. So is Sig Kinsella. Diamond had posted him on the roof of the Amarillo House to cut me down. Kinsella got his from the Swede, Banjo Sorenson, who came to Swayback hunting for him. The only shadow on to-day's doings is that Sorenson died when Kinsella died."

Amy stood against a wall, still silent, her hands behind her, and Larkin glanced at her now. He was through playing cat-and-mouse, and he said, "It would be better if you left us alone for a while, Amy."

She said, "I think not. Some terrible business has brought you here, Dave. I can read it in your face."

He shrugged. "Very well," he said and faced Abbott again. "I want the bank money, Abbott. Where have you hidden Conover's towsack?"

A rush of colour took the greyness out of Abbott's face.

"Are you crazy, Larkin?"

"I watched this house after I left last night," Larkin said. "I had a suspicion that you could get out of that wheel-chair, and I was hoping I might see proof. I saw the man who came riding here, and I followed him afterwards. He was one of Conover's crew, and he's dead and buried. He'd come to report to you, Abbott, to tell you that King Conover would be hitting the town to-day. What other business could have brought an outlaw of the hills to this house last night?"

He thought that Abbott would try bluffing or would seek refuge behind a wild denial, but Abbott only looked at him woodenly and said, "Yes?"

"Conover posted one of his men out here this noon. That man was to be given the loot if anything went wrong, and then, with Conover's bunch split as they made their getaway, any posse that formed was supposed to chase the wrong man. But things didn't work as planned. The whole bunch found themselves in a gun-trap, so the man who ended up with the loot threw it away. Nobody saw him, it seems, when he got rid of it — which means he was free to get rid of it in the most convenient manner at hand. *If I'd have been him,*

265

Abbott, I'd have thrown it on the porch of this house, seeing as you're a secret partner of King Conover's. Now where is it?"

Abbott shook his head, a great deal of his surety gone, and he said, "So you saw Conover's man last night. . . ."

"I should have come back here then and put you under arrest, Abbott. I might have done that, but I had to remember that Amy would suffer too for whatever you'd done. That gave me a bad night, and I'd intended letting you go to-day with a warning. But all that's changed. Now fork over that loot."

Abbott inclined his head and said, "Go and get it for him, Amy."

She vanished from the room; Larkin saw her fumble in a closet that gave off the adjacent dining-room, and she came dragging the towsack and placed it at his feet. He stood staring down at it, and then he lifted his eyes to hers, and he shook his head, not wanting to believe. But he had to say, "So you knew! You knew all the time!"

She kept her eyes away from him, but she said, "No, not until to-day. I was here in the living-room with him when that outlaw threw the sack on to our porch. It was only a moment later that one of the Swayback men caught sight of the fellow and shot him out of his saddle."

"But you must have suspected," Larkin insisted. "You couldn't have lived here in this house with him and not known what sort of game he was playing."

Her gaze met his then, and he saw the defiance in her eyes, and it told him everything. "I began to suspect that he could get out of that wheel-chair whenever it pleased him," she said. "He knew too much of whatever went on for a man who couldn't leave his own house. But do you blame me for staying blind? Whatever he was doing, I knew he was doing as much for me as for himself."

The regret went out of Larkin then, the regret and the last faint hope, and there was only anger left.

He said, "I see it all, now. No wonder you didn't want me to drive Diamond from town. You had a fine deal planned here, Abbott. You had Diamond lined up with you in town, and Conover as your silent partner in the hills, and all the while you were mayor of Swayback and able to run it as you pleased. You'd have made a ruined town out of it, but you'd have gotten fat while you were doing it. I was the last ace you needed to fill your hand. People were getting fed up with the Fandango, so fed up that they were about ready to back old Matt Hobbs in a showdown. So you wanted a new marshal, one with a rep that would put him above suspicion, yet one that would eat out of your hand. You thought I'd do that, because of Amy. It wasn't until last night at dinner that you learned you were wrong about me."

Abbott said, "I thought you'd grown up, Larkin. I thought you'd learned to see an opportunity when one was handed to you. I'd have cut you in, of course. It would have been fat . . . fat. . . . When Cultus Pierce dies, the Boxed-C will go to Amy — and to me. In order to stay in his good graces, I've humoured him. I'd have had a ranch on the flats and a rustler crew in the hills to see that my neighbouring ranchers didn't grow bigger than me. I'd have had a town running wide open, and a cut coming to me out of everything that went into Diamond's till, for he'd have been buying protection at a cheap price, and Diamond was smart enough to see that that was a good deal. I was getting too big for this town, Larkin, so I intended to shape the town to suit my talents. But you couldn't understand that."

"No, Dave," Amy said. "I told you once that you had a touch of the cavalier. I didn't realise then how much that knight-on-horseback stuff meant to you. Sheldon intended to grow, and I wanted to grow with him. And now we've *you* to thank because all of his planning came to nothing."

The edge of her scorn was sharp, but she could never cut him again. He said, "Not long ago your father tried to pass a warning to me. I was too blind to understand him then. I savvy now."

He looked at Abbott, and he said, "I haven't heard the train whistle yet, so it must be late. That means there's still time for you to be on it. Amy, you'll go along with him. That's the worst punishment I can hand either of you — to leave you to each other."

Abbott's long face hardened, and he said, "You've had your say, now I'll have mine. I'm not leaving, Larkin. Diamond's dead; you've said so yourself, and I suppose that Conover's either dead or in jail. Either way, it doesn't matter. Conover won't talk; he's not that kind. That makes the whole deal your word against mine. Supposing you prove that I can climb out of this wheel-chair? My doctor thinks I'm gradually getting better. Who can say how quickly the final cure came?"

Larkin's eyes darkened, and he said, "Be on that train, Abbott. Last night I'd have given you a chance — to-day is different. By rights I ought to be turning you over to a mob. You see, Sig Kinsella talked to me before he died. Kinsella went out cursing; he had a dozen things on his soul that he should have died for, but his anger was because he was dying for the one thing he *didn't* do. He told me, understand, that he'd gotten a pair of broken spurs from you, Abbott, just before you were married. You were going to throw those spurs away, but Kinsella thought they could still be used. That makes you the man Banjo Sorenson should have been hunting — the man who found Sorenson's sister alone in their shack one day. Do you want me to tell the rest of it with Amy standing here listening?"

It was as though he'd planted a fist in Abbott's face; the man sank back limply in the wheel-chair and said, "I knew that Swede for who he was the minute he hit Swayback. He looked enough like his sister. And I knew why he was here. To fool him was the big reason why I've kept to this wheel-chair after I was able to leave it."

Larkin said, "Now, will you be on that train?"

He picked up the tow-sack with his left hand and turned his back on Abbott and started for the doorway, and he was almost out of the room when he dropped the sack and spun around, his right hand going to his hip. His instinct hadn't warned him that Kinsella had been on the roof of the Amarillo House, but he'd been prepared for this, anticipating it. He saw that Abbott's hand had gone under the blanket wrapped around his knees, and appeared again. He saw the gun in Abbott's hand, and he swerved as that gun roared, thunderous in the confines of this room. Larkin's own gun spoke at almost the same instant; Abbott's lead drove a splinter from the framework of the doorway beside Larkin, but the impact of Larkin's bullet half-turned the wheel-chair around, and Amy screamed then and hurled herself between the two men, placing herself before Abbott to protect him; but it was too late.

Larkin said, "I saw the bulge of the gun when I first came into the room. A man who played a game as dangerous as his would be prepared. Half of me was hoping that he'd settle to leave town. The other half was hoping he'd try just what he did. He made the choice for himself, Amy."

She gave him no answer; she had flung herself upon Abbott's body and was sobbing wildly, and with the sound of that in his ears he went out of the house, toting the tow-sack and never looking back, and picked his slow way towards the main street. He walked along blindly, not thinking any more, not caring, and his name was called twice before he heard it. He looked up to see Cultus Pierce walking a horse towards him, and when the cattleman reined short, Pierce said, "I just got word this

morning that you were having your showdown to-day, Dave. I fetched my crew into
town, thinking you might need the backing.
From what I'm told, all the chores are already
done."

Larkin said, "I've just shot it out with Sheldon Abbott. He's dead."

The lift of Pierce's leonine head was his only
show of astonishment. "A personal ruckus,
Dave?"

"No. My last job for this badge," Larkin
said and unpinned the badge and dropped it
into his pocket. "I'm on my way to give it
back to Matt Hobbs. He's all the marshal
Swayback needs now, and he'll want this tin
again. He thinks he's too old for the job, but
it's in his blood just the same."

"Like you and your guns, Dave?"

Larkin shook his head. "They go back into
my war-sack. To stay. Fifteen minutes more
and I'm through. I've only got to give Hobbs
a thousand dollars I collected for Jimmy Davis'
folks, and give him this tow-sack, too. It's
bank loot that King Conover's crew didn't get
away with."

Pierce glanced from the sack to Sheldon
Abbott's house, his leathery old face wooden.
"I think I savvy, Dave. I'm old, but I'm not
blind, and some things I've suspected for a
long time."

Larkin said, "Amy's needing you now. Take her back to the ranch with you, Cultus. Take her back and give her a taste of the wind and the sun, and give her kindness, too. Maybe she'll live to be your daughter again."

"And you, Davy boy?"

"My work here is done," Larkin said. "Matt Hobbs has got the kind of town he can handle, and you'll never have to worry about the high hills again. That just about squares me up all around. There's another debt I owe, but there's no way of paying it. That's always the trouble with the real debts a fellow has."

Pierce extended his hand. "Good-bye, Davy," he said. "Down Texas way they say it, *'Vaya con Dios.'* Go with God."

On the high ridge to the east where Larkin had once rested his horse to look down upon the great tawny bowl of rangeland which Swayback centred, he reined short again, and he saw the town softened by distance, and the steel rails spanning the basin and glinting in the afternoon's sunlight. He might come this way again, he reflected; there were old friends to remember, and the grave of Banjo Sorenson to be kept green, yet he knew that this was sheer whimsey. He had fulfilled his destiny here, and he was looking upon Swayback for the last time.

Yonder was the railroad, and yonder was a town set upon a solid, law-abiding foundation, and these were the beginnings of the changes that would fashion a town into a city. Some day they would give it a name with more dignity, and concrete would replace wooden walks, and he would be part of its legend, and he would be remembered long and pridefully. That, in itself, he supposed was the reward. He wondered then if others of his ilk — the Wyatt Earps and the Bat Mastersons and the Hickoks — had known his kind of loneliness, and he wondered what became of men who helped to bring an end to their own day.

He shrugged these thoughts aside; they smacked of self-pity, and he would have turned away then, putting his back to the town and to his memories of it, but he saw the tiny dust-cloud, the lively banner laid by a rider who came furiously across the rangeland on the trail towards this ridge. He watched with interest and futile speculation; he saw the rider vanish beneath the ridge's overhang, and he was still waiting when the horse bobbed into view over the crest and came towards him. Oddly, he recognised the horse first; it bore the Boxed-C brand and was one of Cultus Pierce's own saddle string; and then he saw that the rider was Melody.

He said, very solemnly, "Is the devil chasing you?"

Dust streaked her face and powdered the cloak she wore. She was breathless, and it took her a struggling moment to find speech, and then she said, "I'm leaving Swayback too. They told me which trail you'd taken. I thought we might as well ride together a ways."

"I'm glad you came," he said. "I've never had the chance to thank you for all you did for me. I had a talk with Judge Bragg before I saddled up. I might have spoken to you when I came to the Fandango yesterday, but it wouldn't have done to have let Diamond know that I knew you."

She said, "Whatever I did for you, it was to repay you for taking that deck of cards from me the night Banjo Sorenson went on trial."

"He meant a lot to you; I could see that," he said. "And now he's dead. That's the reason I didn't come to you before I left town. If the news had reached you about him, I thought you'd want to be alone."

"He was a boy who needed a friend," she said. "Last night I would have married him to keep him from going into the Fandango. I told you that. It wouldn't have been such a bad bargain, not when the other gate was closed. Maybe, in time, I could have learned to love him."

He sensed the truth then, but there was too much of humility in him to accept it, and he said softly, "You're young. You've heard tall tales of a man they call Dave Larkin. Perhaps they've dazzled you. The reputation is one thing — the man is another."

"Your name meant nothing to me," she said. "Not at the first. The night that King Conover was to bring you to Pierce's line shack, I went to Amy Abbott for help. She accused me of being in love with you. When I had time to think about it, I knew that she was right."

He turned that over in his mind, and he said, "Then I have that much to thank her for."

Something of her own kind of pride came into her eyes, and she said, "Cultus Pierce gave me this horse and set me on the trail. He told me that if I rode hard I'd overtake you, and he also told me that I'd likely find you hard to manage. I've never thrown myself at a man before."

He had to smile, but it was only for a moment. He said, "All the years behind have marked me. They say that I fight all of my gun battles over each night. Now there's Nick Diamond and Sheldon Abbott and one or two of Conover's men to come between me and my sleep. You'd rue your bargain before very long."

"I sang you to sleep once," she said. "That night when we were hiding from Conover's men in the foothills. I can sing you to sleep again. But you don't remember that, of course. You were feverish, and you thought I was Amy."

"I was feverish at first," he admitted. "Later I had a lucid moment and I recognised you, and I was happy to be with you. After Pierce took me to his ranch, I couldn't clearly remember everything, but it came back to me in time. I was ashamed then. I thought you belonged to Banjo Sorenson."

The hope came into her eyes, and she said, "Then it was that way with you too? Just for a moment, anyway?"

He looked at her, and it came to him then that they were akin, a rootless pair who'd been carried along by every capricious breeze. They had known loneliness, both of them; they had ridden towards distant hills and distant dreams, but always the mirage had eluded them and they'd had to ride on again. That had been their destiny, and it had made them of a kind. He said now, "What is your name?"

"Melody. There was probably more to it once. I never knew."

He reined close to her and put his arm around her shoulder and looked down into her eyes, and because the invitation was there, he bent and kissed her. He said, "I came here with a dream — a dream of a little land and a house and a few cattle. I had somebody else in mind to share that dream. You know that. Can you believe that I'm glad it's this way instead?"

She said, "I'd have settled for less. Where are we riding?"

"Yonder," he said, and the wave of his hand encompassed all of time and all of distance, everywhere and everything. And so they went stirrup to stirrup, and the trail dipped downwards, and Swayback was lost to them, and the long loneliness was ended.

We hope you have enjoyed this Large Print book. Other Thorndike Press or Chivers Press Large Print books are available at your library or directly from the publishers. For more information about current and upcoming titles, please call or write, without obligation, to:

Thorndike Press
P.O. Box 159
Thorndike, Maine 04986
USA
Tel. (800) 223-6121 (U.S. & Canada)
In Maine call collect: (207) 948-2962

OR

Chivers Press Limited
Windsor Bridge Road
Bath BA2 3AX
England
Tel. (0225) 335336

All our Large Print titles are designed for easy reading, and all our books are made to last.